A Traitor's Vow

A Traitor's Vow

Adventures in Eldnaire
Book Two

Thirzah

The Pearl
PEARLBOOKS.CO

Developmental Editor
BRAD PAUQUETTE

Copy Editor
ALLI PRINCE

Book Designer
ALLI PRINCE

Copyright © 2024 by Thirzah Griffioen

LCCN: 2024917645

Print ISBN: 978-1-960230-10-2
E-book ISBN: 978-1-960230-09-6

This book is dedicated to my family, and all the other readers who begged me for a sequel to Amelia's story. I truly hope you're happy.

And to my brother, who still has yet to read the first book that I dedicated to him.
Yes, I'm calling you out.
Love you!

One

I raised a fist, delivering three sharp knocks to the wooden door in front of me. I had scarcely finished knocking when the door opened, revealing Emperor Kyvir. He wore a simple brown vest over a white shirt—the sleeves of which had been scrunched up to his elbows. Dark half-circles cradled his hazel eyes, and without his crown, his wavy brown curls stuck out in all directions.

The Kyvir who stood before me today looked far different from the Kyvir I usually spoke with—the one who had prince-perfect posture, a permanent polite smile, and always wore a formal suit or uniform. This Kyvir looked more like an overworked barkeeper than an emperor. And yet, in my eyes, he remained as handsome and charming as ever.

Upon meeting my gaze, his haggard face brightened. "Velia! What a coincidence… I was just about to go looking for you. Please, come in."

Kyvir stepped back, allowing me to enter his study. As I stepped inside, I was hit by the acrid smell of ink, and the lighter, herbal fragrance of tea. Straight ahead sat Kyvir's desk, nearly buried in stacks of books and papers. I turned to the right, walking over to the small seating area where four empty, dark leather arm-chairs surrounded a large wooden tea table.

I sat down on the chair to the right of the table, closest to the window, while Kyvir chose the chair beside me, in front of the floor-to-ceiling bookcase. Rain tapped against the window pane behind me, as if politely asking to come inside, and a clock ticked away on the bookshelf.

"Would you like some tea?" Kyvir nodded to the table, where a silver serving tray sat with a teapot, sugar bowl, cream pitcher, teaspoons, and a few teacups with saucers. Fragrant steam escaped from the spout of the teapot, rising toward the wood-paneled ceiling.

"Yes, thank you… I—I'd love some tea."

Kyvir smiled. He stood and picked up the porcelain teapot from the silver tray and tipped it forward. An amber liquid poured from the spout into the teacup closest to me, filling the air with more of that light, herbal fragrance.

I glanced up at Kyvir. "Is that chamomile tea?"

Kyvir poured tea into his own cup before setting the pot back on the tray. "Indeed. It's supposed to calm nerves, but I'm afraid it hasn't worked for me—" he cut himself off with a yawn.

I frowned. "You look exhausted. Did you get any sleep at all last night?"

Kyvir grabbed a sugar cube from the bowl and plopped it into his teacup. "I did fall asleep while looking over some reports, but I'm not sure how long it lasted." He reached forward, taking a teaspoon from the silver tray. He placed the spoon in his cup and started stirring the tea.

The spoon scraped against the bottom of the cup, joining the persistent symphony of rain tapping and clock ticking.

"Kyvir…did something bad happen since we talked yesterday?"

Kyvir stopped stirring, letting his teaspoon fall against the rim of his cup with a loud clink. He pressed his lips together, staring into his teacup. "Velia—I mean, Amelia, tell me…would you despise me if Vilnaria did go to war?"

I straightened in my seat, grasping the arms of the chair. "What? But I thought—"

"Please, don't misunderstand me," Kyvir interrupted, looking up. "I still plan to do whatever it takes to avoid such an outcome, but I…I need to know how you would feel should my efforts fail."

My stomach flipped and thrashed like a fish caught in a net. Dread clawed at my mind, mauling my confidence. "Why? What happened?"

Kyvir picked up his teaspoon and continued stirring.

"I hesitate to tell you since you're supposed to leave for Ivanyar tomorrow—and the last thing you need is something new to worry about—but I think you have a right to know." He looked up. "Three noblemen—Duke Withermur, Marquess Dulket, and Duke Carnell—have begun preparing their troops to leave their territories in the south and west, and head here to Eldnaire."

"What? But why? Surely they don't plan on going to war without your permission!"

Kyvir grimaced. He grabbed the cream pitcher and poured a small amount into his teacup before stirring the liquid again. "Each of these noblemen claim that they have added a large number of new recruits to their guard ranks recently, and simply wish to make use of the royal capital's advanced training facilities...but their true intentions are obvious. Once their troops have arrived, they'll begin pressuring the neutral noblemen to summon their troops as well—all under the guise of training."

My nails dug into the leather arms of my chair. "And then they'll launch an attack?"

"No, they're not quite that brazen yet." Kyvir removed the teaspoon from his cup and placed it back on the serving tray. "But if hundreds of troops gather around Eldnaire, the people will start to become anxious and suspicious."

I lowered my gaze to my teacup, watching as steam rose from the liquid. "I'd feel anxious too if an entire army was standing outside my home."

"Exactly. No one would ever believe that so many soldiers had arrived in the royal city merely to train. They'll begin to spread rumors—anticipating a war. From there, it wouldn't take more than a small spark to start a war between us and Myarna. This is the nobles' way of challenging my authority as the emperor. If enough of them band together, *and* they have the support of the people, I'll have no choice but to acquiesce to their desires. The nobles want war, and my refusal isn't going to stop them."

I frowned, looking up. "What about the soldiers? Surely they don't want to fight..."

Kyvir shook his head. "Once a guard, knight, or soldier has

sworn loyalty to a noble, or to a noble house, that loyalty becomes more important than life itself. The punishment for breaking an oath of loyalty is death."

A shiver lurched down my spine. "Isn't that…extreme?"

"Not when you've sworn on your life to loyally serve a noble family." Kyvir lifted his teacup and saucer from the table, taking a sip.

My nails dug even deeper into the leather armrests. "It's a wonder that anyone ever swears their life then."

Kyvir let out a laugh. "Ah, right… Myarna doesn't have such systems in place, do they?"

I let go of the arms of the chair and clasped my hands, placing them in my lap. "No, we don't. Our military force serves under the Council of Law, whose sole purpose is to protect the country and *all* the people within—not just one person or family. And anyone can join our military—even without prior training or a special background."

"I see…quantity over quality." Kyvir took another sip of his tea.

"Something like that." I glanced down at the ivy-green carpet beneath my scuffed black boots. "But no matter how many troops we have, I doubt we'd be able to fight against your nobles' combined forces…"

Kyvir scowled into his teacup. "Then why? Why would they provoke us?"

I jumped in my seat at Kyvir's scathing tone. "What?"

"Why would Myarna attempt to sabotage our relations with Ivanyar if they *knew* they couldn't stand against us in battle? It doesn't make any sense!"

His eyes met mine and my thoughts turned to the week before. Leon and I had witnessed the attack in the woods. The trail of blood, and a mercenary's pin bearing Myarna's crest near the path—not to mention the abandoned campsite filled with expensive Ivanyaran trade goods—that had catapulted me and Leon into this tangled web of conspiracies and lies. "Well, greed always seems to make people do things that don't make any sense," I murmured.

Kyvir placed his teacup and saucer down on the table with a hard clank. The tea inside sloshed over the rim.

"But do they really think they'd be able to keep their gold if a war was waged against them?" His eyes burned with anger. "Have they any idea what war would mean for them and their people? Do they really think that they would escape the consequences?"

I looked at Kyvir, mouth agape. He was right. Nobody but the Vilnarian nobles had anything to gain from war. Everyone else—Vilnarian and Myarnan citizens alike—had everything to lose. Friends, family, and property. I stared down at my hands. "I... don't know what they think," I murmured.

The rain pelted against the window now, nearly drowning out the ticking clock.

"Right." Kyvir sighed, running a hand over his hair. "I'm sorry, Ve—Amelia. They may be your people, but you aren't responsible for their actions. Speaking of which..." He stood up and crossed the room, stopping by his desk. He grabbed an envelope from the top of a paper stack. "This is the letter I wrote to the leaders in Ivanyar explaining the situation," he walked back, rejoining me in the seating area. "I doubt there's anything I could say that would make the deaths of their ambassadors easier to bear, but I did my best."

Kyvir handed the letter to me, and I studied the crimson wax sealing the letter. The image of a *V* with dragon wings on it had been pressed onto the seal. I set the letter on my lap, and grabbed my teacup and saucer. I lifted the cup to my lips and took a sip. The tea had cooled slightly, and without cream and sugar it had a bitter edge to it. I swallowed another sip before lowering the teacup from my lips. "What will you do about Myarna?"

Kyvir collapsed back into his chair with a sigh, putting a hand to his head.

"I'm not certain," he said. "According to my reports, the troops that the nobles have summoned are due to arrive within two weeks. I should be able to limit their stay to six weeks. So as long as I can keep the people calm and the nobles quiet for that long, everything should turn out fine. But if anyone finds out that Myarna interfered with our relations with Ivanyar, I don't think I'll be able to avoid declaring war on Myarna without damaging my reputation with my people—and losing the respect of every other country on the continent."

I pressed my lips together, studying the golden vines on the rim of my teacup. "Then…we can't afford to let anyone find out."

"Exactly." Kyvir picked up his teacup and saucer. "I sent a letter to the king of Myarna and the Council of Law this morning, requesting that an ambassador or delegate be sent to Eldnaire. In the letter I said that we want to discuss a trade deal, but my hope is that Sir Fern and I can meet with the ambassador in private and question Myarna's actions without anyone raising any suspicions.

If a deal can be struck, then perhaps we can avoid any wars."

As Kyvir spoke, I continued sipping my tea. Finally, I gulped the rest of it down and set my empty teacup back in its saucer on the table. The warm liquid slipped down my esophagus and settled in my stomach like an anvil.

"You're right," I said. "The chamomile doesn't seem to be working."

Kyvir pressed his lips together and shook his head. "I'm sorry, Amelia. This must be quite difficult for you to hear."

I forced the corners of my mouth up into a smile. "I've never been too fond of politics."

Kyvir grimaced back at me, then examined his teacup. The ticking clock and pelting rain seemed to grow louder by the second. My gaze drifted to the shelves. Beside the clock and books, all sorts of figurines, vases, and wood carvings filled the shelves between the books.

"Amelia." Kyvir's voice jerked me out of my thoughts.

"Are you certain that you wish to go to Ivanyar?" His hazel eyes bore into mine. "I'm sure we could figure something else out if you'd rather stay here—"

"No." I let out a deep breath and sat up straight. "No, I couldn't… I promised that I would make up for all the trouble my brother and I have caused you, and I fully intend to keep that promise. I will personally see to it that your message reaches Ivanyar safely." I picked up the letter that Kyvir had given me. "I can't live a lie for the rest of my life, and the Ivanyarans deserve to know what's going on. Besides…if I continue to stay here, Duke Gladik might grow suspicious again."

Kyvir sighed. "Of course, you're right." He cleared his throat. "Speaking of Duke Gladik, has he been giving you and Leon any trouble?"

I winced. "No, not since the festival. I think Kay showing up and telling everyone that Leon and I *are* from Ivanyar truly convinced him that we're the real ambassadors. Now, instead of interrogating us, he simply apologizes every time we meet..."

Kyvir cringed. "Ah, yes. Apologies are the duke's specialty. He doesn't usually make mistakes, but when he does—or thinks he has—he won't let anyone forget it." Kyvir lit up, placing his teacup and saucer back on the table. "Oh, and before *I* forget, I have something I'd like to give you."

Kyvir stood, striding over to his desk. He bent over, grabbing something from behind it. He straightened up and turned around, walking back with a thin, leather scabbard in his hands. The silver hilt of a sword stuck out of the top.

"I was thinking...the journey to Ivanyar might be dangerous. Besides the threat of bandits, there are also wolves, bears, and other wild animals to watch out for." Kyvir stopped in front of me, holding out the sword. "You should take this. For protection."

I stared at the scabbard, imagining the sleek, sharp weapon it housed within. I tore my gaze from the sword, looking up at the emperor. "Kyvir...I appreciate the offer, but I truly have no desire to wield a weapon that takes lives," I said. "Leon and Kay will be accompanying me, and both of them are skilled with a blade, so I believe it'd be best if I left the swordsmanship to the two of them."

"Are you certain?" Kyvir frowned. "You don't want to have the means to defend yourself? Just to be safe?"

"I trust my brother," I smiled. "No matter what comes our way, I know that he'll do his best to protect us."

Kyvir lowered the scabbard. "Very well," he sighed. "But if you won't accept the sword, then please…at least accept this." He placed the sword down on the tea table and reached into his pocket, pulling out a small, black velvet box.

I took the box from him and opened it to reveal a small silver pendant set with a violet stone shaped like a teardrop nestled in the box. My breath caught in my throat.

"It's a necklace," Kyvir said. "I thought it would suit you."

My vision blurred as I stared at the violet pendant. Apart from the shape and size, it was similar to the necklace I had worn to the ball when Leon and I first arrived in Eldnaire. But that necklace had been a gift for *Velia*, the false Ivanyaran ambassador. This necklace was Kyvir's gift to *me*, Amelia. "It's beautiful," I whispered, blinking back tears. "Thank you…"

Kyvir smiled. "I'm glad you like it" He reached for the box, then stopped. "May I?"

I nodded, handing him the box.

The emperor removed the necklace from the box and we both stood. I turned around and lifted my long hair out of the way as Kyvir stepped closer. Kyvir placed the delicate silver chain around my neck, clasping it in the back. I let go of my hair, allowing it to fall back into place as I turned to look at him.

Kyvir's lips smiled, but his eyes didn't as he gazed at me. "Please be safe, Amelia."

"I'll do my best." As I spoke, I found myself staring straight into his eyes—not quite brown and not quite green. The more time

I spent around Kyvir, the more I enjoyed it, and the longer my journey to Ivanyar seemed. Before I could capture my thought, it left my mouth. "I wish I didn't have to leave…"

Kyvir's shoulders dropped. He looked away. "So do I." He stepped back, then flashed me a grin. "But at least you won't have to listen to *another* one of Duke Gladik's thirty-minute apologies after tomorrow, right?"

Two

"*I*'m coming with you."

I blinked as the words left Duke Gladik's smiling lips. The duke wore a dark-green riding jacket with black trim and buttons. His mane of hair glowed as sunlight hit the blond, wind-blown strands. Sitting atop his steed, he looked just like the noble protagonist of an adventure novel.

The rain from the day before had transformed the palace gardens into a spring paradise. The buds lining the trees around the pond had blossomed and started dropping white and pink petals. Flowers—daffodils, hyacinths, crocuses, irises, and primroses—were in full bloom, welcoming spring like a long-lost sister. A sweet, floral scent mingled with the fresh, earthy smell of rain in the cool morning air.

Kay, Leon, and I had just finished loading the saddlebags onto our horses when the duke rode up the side path, joining us at the gate at the back of the palace gardens.

My body shivered against the cool morning air and my knees wobbled beneath me as the duke's words sank in. My mouth parted, but no sound left my lips. When I first saw the duke approaching I had worried that he wanted to make one last apology before we left, but this was worse. *Far* worse.

Leon laughed. He crossed his arms, glancing at me. "That really isn't necessary, Duke Gladik. It'll take us a full two weeks to get to Ivanyar's border from Eldnaire, and we don't need—"

"I insist," the duke interrupted. His brow lowered as he clutched his horse's reins. "My conscience—and my honor as a Von Gladik—demand that I atone for my behavior, so I plan to escort you and ensure that you arrive home unharmed. I may not look it, but I have some experience with camping and traveling." He looked around at the three of us. "And before you start to protest, you should know that I won't be persuaded otherwise."

My brain began to buzz like a colony of bees had taken up residence inside my mind. I placed a hand on my head to try to silence it.

"Well, if you insist, then I certainly won't stand in your way," Leon said. "We'd be *happy* to have you join us, Duke."

I whipped around to look at Leon. "We *would?*" I choked out.

Leon winked at me. "Of course we would. It's all right with you too, right Kay?"

Kay glanced at Leon and shrugged his broad shoulders. He wore a simple, short-sleeved olive tunic, which drew far more attention to the bulging muscles on his arms than the fur cloak he'd worn when we first met at the spring festival. His long, dark hair had been tied back, clearly exposing the scar in the center of his forehead. I'd been surprised when he offered to accompany Leon and me to Ivanyar, but also quite relieved. Kay reminded me a little of Kyvir with his gentle, eloquent way of speaking and regal confidence. And if *I* couldn't talk sense into Leon, then Kay—a mountain in the form of a man—certainly could.

"The duke is more than welcome to accompany us, but we need to get going soon," Kay said. "We've got a long journey ahead of us."

My stomach sank like a boulder in a pond. So much for talking sense. "But the duke—"

Leon stepped over to me, patting my shoulder with one hand, and handing me my horse's reins with his other. "The duke will be *helpful* if we run into any bandits on our way home," he finished for me. "Here Lia, do you need help mounting your horse? It's at least a hundred times bigger than you, after all," Leon laughed.

I glared at my brother. "Very funny." I lowered my voice to a whisper as I walked around the side of my horse, out of Duke Gladik's direct line of sight. "Leon why—"

Leon waved my words away. "I'll explain later," he murmured. "Now here, let me help you." He reached under my arms and boosted me up, allowing me to pull myself up onto the saddle. I gripped the reins with both hands as my heart skipped like a stone thrown across a pond.

Between Leon's confidence and Kay's aloofness, I was outnumbered. But if Leon's confidence was misplaced—as it usually was—and Duke Gladik found out the truth, he'd return to Vilnaria and spread the news to everyone. There wouldn't be a country on this side of the continent that wouldn't want us imprisoned or dead.

I watched as Leon mounted his own horse with the skill and agility of a cavalry soldier. His white linen shirt contrasted sharply with his raven hair and dark eyes. He also had a bright smile on his face—which I had long ago learned to interpret as a warning sign. Leon was like a hunting dog. Eager, talented, dangerous, and impossible to understand—even when he spoke.

We rode for most of the day, only stopping to water and rest the horses. That evening, Duke Gladik and I sat around a fire eating while Kay and Leon went to gather enough wood to last us through the night. Throughout the day's ride, and even while we worked to set up camp, Kay rarely spoke and seldom smiled—the complete opposite of the duke sitting across from me.

"I still can't believe I truly thought that you and your brother were frauds," Duke Gladik said, glancing at me as he tore a piece of bread from a loaf he had brought with him. "I could have completely ruined your reputations with my actions and accusations—so I must apologize again."

I grimaced, reaching into my bag and taking out a green apple. Leon and I were perfectly capable of ruining our own reputations. "Please…don't worry about it, Duke Gladik. You've already apologized many, *many* times today, and I'm sure you had good reason to suspect us." My stomach twisted like a turned ankle as I spoke. Accepting his apologies felt like stealing bread from a starving beggar.

The duke nodded. "Yes, I suppose I did have my reasons. But now that I think about it, my suspicions made no sense—having fake ambassadors show up at the palace would have completely undermined their plan."

I lowered my apple from my lips. "Their plan? Whose plan?"

The duke leaned forward, lowering his voice. "Well, you see, a few weeks ago, I was made aware of a plot by the pro-war faction of Vilnarian nobles. Their plan was to frame Myarna for the murder of Ivanyar's ambassadors, which would lead to—"

"Wait," I blinked, holding up my free hand. "You're saying that the nobles' goal was to frame Myarna?"

He nodded, swallowing a bite of bread. "Yes, you see, they planned to hire mercenaries to kill the ambassadors on their way to Eldnaire. After that, they would plant some sort of false evidence to make it seem as if the mercenaries were sent by Myarna—which in turn would give us a strong reason to go to war with our northern neighbors."

My thoughts jumped to the mercenary's brooch Leon had found in the middle of the road. Had it been dropped on purpose?

I swallowed hard. "And...you're...you're sure about that? You're sure their plan was to frame *Myarna* for the death of the ambass—I mean, our death?"

The duke pursed his lips, lowering his head. "Of course, I didn't want to believe it...and when my aide first informed me of the conspiracy, I had my doubts." He sighed, his shoulders slumping over. "But then I overheard a conversation between two nobles at the palace, and I couldn't deny it any longer..."

I set my apple down next to me, balancing it on the log I sat on. Nausea jabbed at my stomach like a knife, my toes curled over within my leather boots. It had to be true then. Myarna was the real target all along.

"You're…absolutely certain?"

"Unfortunately so," Duke Gladik said, looking up. "Once I confirmed it, I reported the plot to the highest authority—and he said he'd have someone look into it." He stared at the bread in his hand. "I…know it's shameful of me, but I didn't truly believe anything would come of my report. I suspected that some of the more powerful and influential nobles were secretly in favor of war, so I was certain that their plan would succeed." He shook his head, letting out a chuckle. "I'm sure you can imagine the shock I felt when you and your brother arrived at the palace safe and sound. I was convinced that you had to be frauds hired by the nobles!" He laughed long and hard, his shoulders bouncing up and down.

I clutched my necklace. My heart beat faster than a galloping horse, and my body shuddered as ripples of anxiety spread throughout my chest, arms, and legs.

Across from me, Duke Gladik continued to laugh, wiping a tear from his eye as he smiled at me. "Although, now that I'm saying it out loud, it's rather obvious how absurd that is. What good would having false ambassadors do?"

My tongue turned to stone within my mouth. Memories flooded through my mind as I stared at the fire dividing us. The brooch—the conversation I had with Kyvir and the empress dowager about Myarna and their possible motives, even telling Kyvir that Myarna was filled with greed…

Every step Leon and I took since entering Vilnaria had played right into the hands of Vilnaria's pro-war nobles. I had single-handedly led Kyvir, Marta, Sir Fern, and everyone else to believe that Myarna had tried to sabotage relations between Ivanyar and Vilnaria. Even now, soldiers were on their way to gather in Eldnaire, and if even the tiniest whisper arose to accuse Myarna of wrongdoing, there'd be no saving my homeland.

"Miss Velia? Is everything all right? You look paler than usual…"

I looked up from the flickering flames. "I…yes, of course." I forced the corners of my mouth up into a smile. "I'm sorry, it's just…I can't believe that the nobles would be willing to go so far… All to start a war."

Duke Gladik frowned. "Ordinarily they wouldn't have to. The late emperor had planned to conquer the entirety of the north during his reign, but due to his sudden death, he never got to accomplish his goals."

I nodded. "And Ky—Emperor Kyvir, has no desire to go to war. He's the complete opposite of his father." As I spoke, my ears picked up the sound of crunching leaves.

Leon entered the clearing with a large glass jar full of yellow springberries, followed by Kay who held an armload of wood.

"That's it, I'm convinced you can't go more than fifteen minutes without talking about your lover," Leon smirked as he and Kay joined us by the fire.

The heat from the fire merged with the heat in my cheeks. "Leon, don't say that! The emperor is *not* my lover."

Leon plopped down next to me, knocking my apple off the log. "So you admit that you were talking about him."

I shot Leon a glare, letting go of my necklace to grab the fallen apple. "Duke Gladik and I were just discussing how different Emperor Kyvir is from his late father," I brushed the apple off with my shirt sleeve.

Kay set the wood down in a pile a few feet away from the fire. "That's likely due to the empress dowager's influence," he said, taking a seat on the other side of Leon.

I smiled. "She's a kind woman."

"Indeed, I quite enjoyed meeting her. Though, from what I understand, her kindness toward the north comes from her own… experience," Kay's gentle voice held a hint of bitterness. He gestured for the jar of berries that Leon had placed on the ground in front of himself.

Leon picked the jar up, snatching a handful of berries with his free hand before giving it to Kay. "What do you mean?"

"It's a rather…sensitive topic to discuss," Duke Gladik interjected. "In Eldnaire—and especially in the palace—it's an unspoken rule that we don't speak of the empress dowager's past."

Leon glanced around. "It seems to me that we're not in Eldnaire, or the palace for that matter, so it shouldn't be a problem if you tell us a little."

The duke frowned. "It's not really my place to discuss such things."

Leon turned to Kay, who was shoveling springberries into his mouth. "In that case, what do *you* know?"

Kay swallowed, resting the jar on his knee. His dark eyes reflected the flickering flames of the fire. "Sir Fern mentioned that the empress dowager belonged to the former Eldnairian royal family," he said. "She was their eldest princess and married the late emperor for political and personal reasons after Eldnaire was conquered by Vilnaria and her parents were killed."

I gaped at Kay. "What?"

"It's not quite that simple," Duke Gladik said. "There's a long history between Vilnaria and the former royal state of Eldnaire. But it's true... The empress dowager accepted the late Emperor Hykil's proposal for the sake of her people, not for herself."

Kay nodded. "And since the late emperor had plans to conquer the north during his reign, he eventually moved Vilnaria's capital to Eldnaire, closer to his targets."

My thoughts turned to the empress dowager, the picture of elegance and poise. When speaking about the late emperor, her face never showed even the slightest hint of emotion. Whatever she felt toward her deceased husband, she hid it behind a mask stronger than iron. A stark contrast to Kyvir, who clearly mourned the loss of his father, even if he didn't agree with his methods of ruling the empire.

"She must have celebrated just as much as the rest of the north when the last emperor died," Leon said.

I choked on my own saliva, gaze snapping to my brother. "Leon! You really can't say things like that!"

Leon shrugged. "Why not? It's true. I mean, in Myarna—from what I heard—there was an impromptu festival that lasted an entire week. Singing, dances, performances... I doubt anyone could have been happier if they were giving out gold."

Duke Gladik's face paled. "They *celebrated* the late emperor's death?"

Leon hummed, tilting his head to the side. "Well, not his death per se, but what it *symbolized* to them," he grabbed some berries from the jar Kay held. "The death of the emperor meant safety and freedom—even if it was only temporary. For years Myarnans have been watching as Vilnaria's forces march farther and farther north. And back when Eldnaire fell, they knew they'd be next. So is it any wonder that they were happy?"

The duke's brow lowered. "Still...death is something that should never be celebrated," he murmured.

Leon raised an eyebrow. "I'm guessing you're not too fond of executions then."

Duke Gladik stiffened. "No, I'm not fond of them at all."

I shuddered. "Neither am I."

Leon smiled. "Well, in any case...when we travel through Myarna, you may want to refrain from telling any Myarnans that you're a pure-blooded Vilnarian, Duke Gladik—just to be safe."

Duke Gladik's eyes widened. "Would they harm me just for being Vilnarian?"

Leon shrugged. "Well, I'm sure they could find a few other reasons if they tried hard enough."

"Enough, Leon," I snapped. "Let's not talk about this anymore."

Leon frowned. "Why not? It's true."

I squeezed the apple I held in my hands, swallowing hard. "Just stop it, okay? Now isn't the time."

Leon sighed. "Okay, fine... Whatever makes you happy." He popped a few more berries into his mouth.

Duke Gladik's face was still noticeably pale while Kay stared into the dying flames of the fire, his hand hovering over the jar of berries. With each crackle and pop of the fire, my stomach

21

thrashed and turned like a fish caught in a net.

I had been wrong. Vilnaria's nobles had been at fault all along, but I had pointed a finger at Myarna—my own country—without a thorough investigation—and to a *foreign ruler* no less. Did that mean that I had committed treason?

I sighed, closing my eyes. My mistakes and failures were starting to pile up into a mountain of guilt that I couldn't climb. My home—my parents—were in danger because of *my* actions. Somehow, I had to find a way to fix everything—before it was too late.

Three

*B*etween the twigs and rocks digging into my back through my blanket and the guilt plaguing my mind, I hardly slept that night. Instead, I stared up through the gaps in the tree branches and leaves at the star-filled sky above. Myarna had been framed. But what was I supposed to do with that information? Continue to Ivanyar and deliver Kyvir's letter as planned or return to Eldnaire and inform Kyvir of my mistake? He had written his letter under the impression that Myarna was to blame for sabotaging relations with Ivanyar—not his own countrymen. But what excuse could we give to the duke to justify turning back?

By the time morning finally came and the sun rose, my head and back ached. Somehow I had to find a way to tell Leon and Kay what was going on—without the duke overhearing. Kay appeared to know quite a bit concerning the histories of the Vilnarian Empire, Myarna, and Ivanyar—more than I had expected. Perhaps he would have some idea of what to do.

Once everyone was awake, the four of us packed up camp, brushed down our horses, and set off again, serenaded by birdsong.

Around midmorning we stopped by a stream just off the main path to our right, where we could water our horses. After tying the horses to the trees closest to the stream, I leaned against a nearby trunk, watching as my horse drank the clear water. Kay stood between me and the horses, examining our map, while Leon sat on a patch of moss next to the water and munched on the last of our apples. Duke Gladik excused himself, hopped over the stream, and took off deeper into the forest to relieve himself.

Finally, this was my chance.

I waited until I no longer heard the shifting and crunching of leaves under the duke's boots, then turned to Leon and Kay. "Hey, so I—"

"Since we decided to pack light, we're going to need to stop at the next town for more food and to switch out our horses," Kay interrupted, eyes glued to the map. "The nearest town is Averndale, so we'll head there."

Leon looked up from his apple, grinning. "Averndale, you say? In that case, Lia, maybe we should stop by our house and pay Mother and Father a quick visit."

I glared at him. "Do *you* want to explain to our parents what's happened and what we're doing right now? Because I certainly don't. Mother might faint, and Father would lecture us for the next three days, at least!"

Leon shrugged. "They're already going to be mad since we were only supposed to be gone for a week."

"Exactly, so I see no need to make things worse." I let out a breath. "Besides, thanks to *you*, Duke Gladik is traveling with us, and if he finds out that we were lying after all—"

"Look, the only reason I agreed to let Gladik come was because it would have looked pretty suspicious if we refused. And, even if we did refuse, you know how mulishly stubborn he is. He probably would have just followed us anyway." Leon took another bite from his half-eaten apple.

I frowned down at my boots. "But still…"

"No, in this case, I believe that Leon is right," Kay folded the map and stuffed it into his pocket. "Our goal is to establish peace and avoid war. So if we want our mission to succeed, it's best that we do everything in our power to not give Duke Gladik any reason for suspicion. Since he's traveling with us instead of trailing us from a distance, we'll be able to keep a closer eye on him."

I brushed some dark strands of hair out of my face and behind my ears. Kay's explanation made sense in a way, but the idea of keeping up the act of being an Ivanyaran ambassador the entire way to Ivanyar made my stomach twist. "And you really think we can deceive him for the entire trip?"

"Have you talked to the man?" Leon scoffed. "He's not exactly the brightest star in the sky."

Kay shook his head. "Don't be too quick to write him off. The duke is young, inexperienced, and somewhat naive, but he's not a fool. We'll have to be extremely wary of him."

"I think you're giving him too much credit." Leon snorted. "He's nothing but a wealthy snob who needs to learn how to keep his nose out of other people's business."

"You're rather quick to cast judgment on a man who you hardly know."

Leon narrowed his eyes at Kay. "Are you saying that you *do* know him?"

"I'm merely well acquainted with the details of his situation," Kay replied. "Nothing more."

Before Leon could respond, I jumped in. "Well, before he comes back, there's something I have to tell you both," I glanced in the direction Duke Gladik had wandered off in. "Last night, the duke told me that Myarna—"

Kay's gaze snapped up. "Wait a moment... Do you hear that?"

"Hear what—"

Kay held up a hand and frowned.

I tilted my head, listening. Off in the distance, a woodpecker thumped away at a tree. The sound echoed through the forest, mingling with the sound of rushing water from the stream. A fly buzzed by the horses. One of them swished its tail, driving the fly away.

Suddenly, all the horses stopped, raising their heads as their ears twitched, turning in different directions. Over the rushing water, I heard the faint sound of leaves crunching underfoot somewhere in the woods—in the opposite direction that Duke Gladik had disappeared.

Leon stood. "Is someone coming?" he asked.

Kay put a finger to his lips. "Wait..."

I listened again, but the crunching had stopped.

Kay's frown deepened. His hand slid to his side, hovering over his sword's hilt. "Everyone, grab your weapons. Something is off."

My eyes widened. "Our weapons? What do you mean? Is—"

Something zipped past my head and thudded into the tree behind me. An arrow. I let out a shriek, jumping to the side.

Our horses pawed the ground, yanking at their tethers. The sound of crunching leaves grew louder and faster. Three figures wearing black emerged from behind the trees about fifteen feet away, blocking our way back to the main path. The two men in front carried swords. The man in the back held a bow, and was already reaching for another arrow from his quiver. Kay and Leon jumped in front of me, their swords unsheathed.

"Take out the archer first. Leon, cover me," Kay said before charging forward. The men in front lunged at him.

Kay dodged the strike from the man on the left as a half-eaten apple hit the man on the right, square in the face, eliciting a strangled grunt.

"Hey!" Leon shouted, brandishing his sword. "The fight's over here."

The man who had been assaulted by the apple growled and lunged at Leon. Their swords clashed. The metallic clang rang out and echoed through the wood.

The other swordsman in black turned his attention toward me. My feet were firmly planted on the ground, a scream stuck halfway up my throat as he approached. Panic exploded within my mind, and only one thought remained. I was about to die.

The man lunged at me, and my body reacted before my mind, dodging to the right. The man swung and I jumped back as the sword swiped at the fabric covering my shoulder. I had a hunting knife somewhere—but where? My satchel? My sad-

27

dlebag? I needed to attack. To fight for my life.

The man struck, swung, and stabbed at me as I dodged, ducked, and jumped out of reach, edging closer and closer toward the stream. He grunted, slashing at me again. I dashed to the side, crying out as pain stung my upper arm. I stumbled and tripped, falling as the man took another swing at me, just missing my side. I slammed against the forest floor, pain shooting through my head and arm.

The ground beneath me shook. The sound of the water rushing grew louder in my ears as I stared at the man standing over me. His cloak hid most of his face, and a scarf covered his mouth. I was going to die. Not at the gallows, and not in the Vilnarian palace. In the woods, just minutes away from my hometown.

I shut my eyes as the sword swung down. A loud clank resounded, ringing in my ears. I opened my eyes. Leon stood in front with his back toward me, his sword locked against the other man's weapon.

"Leon?" I gasped. My vision swirled as I sat up.

Leon grunted, pushing his sword against the other man's blade, forcing it upward. The man jumped back and ducked, removing his sword from the deadlock. Leon stumbled forward, and before he could recover, the man swung at Leon again. I heard a "*thwip*," and Leon cried out, stumbling back and tripping over my foot. He fell to the ground next to me.

The other man swung again, but stopped mid-swing, eyes wide. His sword dropped to the ground, and his body followed, collapsing in a heap at our feet.

Duke Gladik stood over him, panting. He grasped a sword in

both hands, the tip covered in crimson.

"Miss Velia, Mr. Lyon," he panted. "Are you all right?"

The duke's voice snapped me out of my daze. I turned to look at Leon. His face had turned pale, his breathing shallow. His shirt had been slashed, and a thin red line formed on the white fabric around the long slit. I blinked. The red stripe across his chest grew. I blinked again. It grew bigger. My brother grew paler.

"Quickly, he's losing blood!"

Kay's voice sliced through my confusion. He dropped to his knees next to Leon, ripping the bottom of his undershirt. An arrow stuck out of Kay's right shoulder. I inhaled a breath so large I choked on it, coughing. My vision blurred.

A metallic smell invaded my nose, and my stomach retched. I turned away, gagging. My body shook as if it were the dead of winter. The image of my brother—him stumbling, falling, and then the red—played over and over again in my mind. I couldn't look. I couldn't see. I couldn't admit that it was real. My brother was dying. Maybe he was already dead. I didn't want to know. I didn't want to see. I didn't want to feel.

A hand grabbed my arm. "Miss Velia."

I tried to wrench my arm out of Duke Gladik's grasp. "No," I coughed out. "No…"

A canteen touched my lips. I grabbed it with my free hand, gulping water down. It soothed my throat but couldn't wash away the images in my mind.

"We need to get him to a physician," I heard Kay's voice.

"Is there a town nearby?" Duke Gladik asked. "Where should we go?"

29

My gaze snapped up. "Averndale." The word left my mouth in a hoarse whisper. I cleared my throat. "Bring him to Averndale. To our parents' house. They can help."

People rushed to the side of the streets of Averndale as we thundered down the stone sett road toward my parents' house. In any other situation, I'd be thrilled to ride down the familiar streets toward my childhood home.

Compared to the tall, drab, timber and stone houses of Vilnaria's royal capital, Eldnaire, the bright, redbrick houses lining the streets of Averndale's largest residential district stood out against the gray streets and small, flower-filled, verdant lawns.

Red. My mind buzzed with unwanted images of the black-clad mercenaries, Kay's injured shoulder, and the blood staining my brother's white linen tunic.

I glanced back at Kay, who rode with Leon on his horse, but averted my eyes when they threatened to glance at his shoulder and the arrow still embedded within. "We're nearly there," I said over the clopping of hooves on stone.

He nodded, his lips pressed together.

I swallowed, wincing from the bitter taste of bile that lingered in my mouth. Up ahead, I spotted my parents' house, a redbrick townhome with dark-green shutters. I stopped my horse in front of it, motioning for the others to do the same. I dismounted, my boots hitting the stone with a thud.

"What on—Amelia? Is that you?" a woman's voice called out.

I turned. My mother stood in the doorway of the house, her long, black-and-gray peppered hair was tied up into a messy knot on the top of her head. She wore a deep-red dress with a white apron tied over it, and her hands were stained black with ink.

Water rushed to my eyes like a river, blurring my vision and threatening to pour out like rain. "Mother!" I ran like a child, my leather boots slapping the stone pathway as I sprinted to her. I wrapped my arms around her, ignoring the pain in my arm as the tears rolled down my cheeks.

"Amelia…" My mother pulled me closer, holding me tight. "Where have you been? We were so worried…" her voice broke as she spoke.

I swallowed, pulling back. "Mother—Leon. Leon…he's been…we need a physician now!"

Four

"Your son lost a large amount of blood, but the cut wasn't deep enough to cause any severe issues," the physician, Dr. Kander, told my father as the two of them stepped out of the hallway and entered the front room where I sat with Duke Gladik and Kay. "I've stitched him up, so as long as the wound doesn't become infected, he'll make a full recovery."

I unclenched my jaw and let out a deep breath, collapsing against the back of my seat as Dr. Kander finished speaking.

My father nodded as he and the physician walked farther into the room. Father had rushed home after a neighbor delivered the news about Leon's injury, so he still wore his "library clothes"—a tan suit jacket with a white undershirt, matching tan pants, and a green necktie. His slicked-back, dark-gray hair stuck out in a few places, and his hands trembled, but overall my father appeared as dignified and respectable as ever. "Thank you, Dr. Kander. I appreciate the haste in which you arrived."

Dr. Kander smiled. "That's part of my job." He looked back toward the hallway. "Though I'd say my presence was basically useless with Vya tending to him. Your wife could have been a physician herself, if she wanted to be."

"The skills of a worried mother have no equal, certainly," my father said.

Dr. Kander glanced at me and the others. I sat on a cracked, brown-leather couch. Duke Gladik sat in an old, velvet-cushioned armchair to the right of me in the corner of the room, near the front door. Kay remained standing on the opposite side of me, leaning against the floral wallpaper, his injured shoulder wrapped in bandages. His jaw was clenched and his hands were in his pockets.

"Now then..." Dr. Kander began, "it seems you have other matters to deal with, so I'll show myself out. But you know where to find me."

My father nodded and Dr. Kander left the house.

As the door closed behind the physician, my father turned to look at all of us, his gaze settling on me as he crossed his arms. "So, does anyone care to explain why my son was cut across his chest with a sword?"

I winced. Anger dripped from his words like water from melting icicles. He had scolded Leon and me plenty of times in the past, but this was different. I had never heard this tone from my quiet, mild-mannered father. Averting my gaze, I glanced around the front room. Across the room, behind my father, sat our newer set of dark-green upholstered furniture, a coffee table, and the mantel over the fireplace where our family had spent most winter nights talking, laughing, and reading. A few pieces of unused firewood still lay in the corner next to the mantel. To my right, the early afternoon sunlight poured through the windows on either side of the front door, casting large squares of light on the wooden floor.

"You and Leon were only supposed to be gone for five days—if that—but it's been well over a week now," my father continued, raising his voice. "And not *once* did you send us word. Your mother and I weren't even sure if you were alive!"

I swallowed hard. "I'm so sorry, father... We weren't able to contact you because we ran into some trouble in Vilnaria—"

"I should have known," my father interrupted, shaking his head. "I knew it was a mistake to allow the two of you to go there—I should have gone myself or paid Dante to do it. Was it the guards? Did they attack Leon?"

"No, Mr. Huld," Kay spoke up. "We were attacked by Vilnarian mercenaries in the woods near this town."

"Vilnarian mercenaries?" My father blinked at Kay. "Here? Why would you be attacked by mercenaries?"

My gaze flitted to Kay's stony face. I never had a chance to tell him what Duke Gladik had revealed the night before, so how did he know that the mercenaries were Vilnarian—and not Myarnan?

I turned back to my father and swallowed hard. "It's...a long story."

My father's eyes narrowed. "Then I suggest you start talking, Amelia Lorraine Huld."

"On our way to Eldnaire, Leon and I witnessed a murder."

My father's eyes widened. "What?"

"We were in the woods, heading toward Eldnaire, when we

saw three people flee across the path ahead of us. They were being chased by the mercenaries, and…" I cleared my throat. "There was nothing we could do to help, so we kept walking. But then we saw smoke coming from the same direction those people had fled from, and Leon insisted we investigate…so we did. The smoke was coming from a campsite, and there were a bunch of expensive trade goods from Ivanyar—furs even."

"Did you report your findings to the authorities?"

I frowned. "No—I mean, that *was* the plan. Leon and I took as many of the goods as we could carry, and I fully intended to turn all of it over to the guards the moment we arrived in Eldnaire. But before we could, the emperor's highest-ranked adviser, Sir Fern, found us and assumed that Leon and I were ambassadors from Ivanyar because we were wearing the furs we found. It turned out that the people we had seen were the *real* ambassadors."

My father stared at me as if I had just slapped him and spit in his face. "And you didn't tell that man the truth?"

I sat up straight in my seat. "I tried! I really tried, Father! But Leon started pretending we were the ambassadors, and I thought that if I told the truth we'd both be killed for lying to a noble…"

My father groaned, placing his hand over his face. "Of all the—what happened after that? Were you discovered?"

I pressed my lips together, playing with my fingers. "Well, yes and no… The emperor, Sir Fern, and the empress dowager found out who we really are, and they asked for our help."

My father took a step back. "The Emperor of Vilnaria asked *you* for help?"

"Well, I…I volunteered because I felt guilty for lying and pre-tending to be an ambassador."

My father opened his mouth, then closed it and shook his head. "Never mind…" he muttered. "So, why were you attacked by mercenaries?"

I glanced at Duke Gladik. He glared down at his lap, his jaw clenched. I sank down in my seat and looked away. He had to be angry. Furious, even. Kyvir, Sir Fern, Kay—we'd all spent so much time and energy trying to fool him into believing we were ambassadors, only for the truth to come spilling out like water from a fountain.

I looked up at my father. "It turns out that some of the Vil-narian nobles are looking for an excuse to go to war against Myarna. They're the ones who hired mercenaries to kill the real ambassadors, and I'm sure they're the ones who tried to have us killed as well."

My father watched me the entire time I spoke, his arms crossed, and his lips pressed into a firm line as the color drained from his face. "So, you're saying that Vilnaria plans to finally con-quer the north?" he asked.

"It's really only a few of the nobles who want war," I said. "The emperor is actively doing everything in his power to avoid conflict between our countries."

"And you really believe that?" Father scoffed.

"Of course I do." I reached up, grasping my necklace. "I trust Emperor Kyvir."

Saying those words out loud filled me with warmth. An image of Kyvir's wavy curls, smiling lips, and hazel eyes entered my mind, replacing the images of Leon collapsed on the forest floor and bleeding.

"I see." Father's eyes pierced mine, sharp as pins. "If what you're saying is true, then we have no other options." My father turned, walking over to the mantelpiece. He started taking down the family heirlooms, setting them on the coffee table. "A cart will have to be rented, and I'll need to go down to the market and buy some storage crates…"

I frowned as he turned a blue vase over, shaking a few coins out onto the table. "Father, what are you doing?"

Father looked up from the coins. "Packing. And you should do the same. As soon as I can get our affairs here settled, we're taking a carriage to port Sorvin. From there, we'll take a boat to Regol and stay with your cousins until we can find a new place of our own."

My eyes widened. "What?"

My father looked out the window. "We're not going to sit around and wait for war to drive us out of our homes." He let out a breath, rolling his shoulders back. "We're leaving the peninsula now, before it's too late."

I shot to my feet. "Wait, Father—the war isn't going to happen! The emperor doesn't know that his nobles were trying to frame Myarna for murder, but once I return to Eldnaire and tell him what's going on, then the war will be stopped—"

"No one can stop the Vilnarian Empire, Amelia," he interrupted. "How many villages, towns, cities, kingdoms, and countries have they conquered in the past?"

I shook my head. "This is different, Father. The emperor—"

"*Nothing* is different, Amelia. History *always* repeats itself." My father grabbed the coins from the table, dropping them into a small money pouch that clinked each time he added a coin. "The Vilnarians will continue to take everything from us until the day their empire falls. The only thing we can do is wait until that day comes."

Frustration burned through my veins like fire, turning my patience to ash. "It's not what you think, Father. Emperor Kyvir wants nothing but peace. If we work together, we can avoid the pain and suffering of war. But running and waiting for problems to solve themselves won't change a thing!" I burst out, placing a hand on my chest. "Right now, I have a chance to fix this situation—"

"Your *chance* nearly *killed* your brother," Father snapped, narrowing his eyes. "Listen to me, Amelia. What you and your brother did was not only foolish and dangerous, but treasonous. If the Council of Law were to find out about this, they'd send you and Leon straight to the dungeons—or worse! Far worse…"

I stepped forward. "I know, Father, but that's why I have to fix this and—"

"No!" Father yelled. "You're done, Amelia! No more adventures, and no more playing the hero. Your place is with your family, and your family is leaving Averndale as soon as possible!"

My fists clenched. "But we can't abandon everyone!"

Father tilted his head. "Are you on the Council of Law?"

"No, but—"

"Do you have ties to the royal family?"

"That's not—"

38

"No, you don't," he continued. "But you do have a tie to *this* family. To your mother, brother, and myself. We love you, Amelia—*I* love you." He lowered his voice. "And sometimes love means making difficult decisions. So tell me, who do *you* love? Your family, or the strangers who will kill you if they ever find out about what you've done?"

My lips parted as I stared at my father. "Of course I love you, but—"

"Good, then act like it." Father pointed to Duke Gladik and Kay. "See your acquaintances out and start packing." He walked toward the front door.

"No!" I shouted.

Father whirled around, eyebrows raised. "Excuse me?"

I swallowed, grabbing fistfuls of my skirt. "I won't run, Father. Not when there's a chance that I can fix this. You've always taught Leon and I to take responsibility for our actions, and that's what I intend to do."

"Don't use my words to justify this stupidity," Father scowled. "You're not a spy, and you're not a soldier. You're my daughter."

I shook my head. "I understand—"

"No, Amelia, you obviously don't!" He pointed at me. "You think that you can single-handedly save Myarna from war, but you can't. It takes an *army* to fight a war, not naive optimism."

"Well, I can't just give up!"

"That's the type of thinking that kills people. It's the type of thinking that nearly killed your brother today, Amelia!" Father sighed, rubbing his forehead. "Your mother and I thought we raised you to make wise decisions, but perhaps we didn't do quite as well as we had hoped."

His words stung like I had been shoved face-first into a hornet's nest. Tears pricked at the corner of my eyes. I opened my mouth, then closed it, lowering my gaze to the floor.

Father stepped over to the front door and opened it, looking back at me. "Now, I'm going to the market to pick up some extra crates. By the time I return, I want all these people *out* of my house, understood?"

Before I could respond, the front door slammed shut behind my father. I stood in the middle of the front room, staring at the door.

"So I was right."

My shoulders slumped as I turned to face the duke. I had nearly forgotten about him. "Duke Gladik…"

The duke stared at me, his face pale. "You *are* a false ambassador."

I winced. "Duke Gladik, I'm so sorry, but I couldn't tell you. The emperor—"

"The emperor…forced me to leave the ball on the first night," the duke interrupted. "He instructed me to apologize to you both, and that time when you were in his office… He made me apologize and sent me away." The duke's voice faded into a whisper. "All of that…was a lie. All of you knew I was right, but you said *nothing*."

All the guilt I'd felt over the past several days came rushing back like a flooded river, threatening to sweep me away and drown me in regret. I stepped forward. "I'm so sorry, Duke. I really am… But the emperor really did have a good reason for—"

"For what?" he snapped. "Lying to us all? Destroying what

40

little trust he had among his most loyal nobles? I won't accept any excuses!" The duke's nostrils flared. "The emperor of all people should know that he cannot play with the lives of his subjects and expect to get away with it!"

I stiffened. "Duke Gladik, Kyvir is doing his very best to help everyone—"

The duke scoffed. "And he believes that lying to their faces is helpful?"

I opened my mouth to speak, but the duke cut me off.

"Lies are not tools to be used when it is convenient. They are weapons—weapons that destroy lives!"

"You don't need to lecture me, Duke," I said through clenched teeth. I placed a hand over my heart. It beat hard. Hard and fast. "I'm aware that what my brother and I did was wrong—and I am so sorry—but I can't change the past or undo what was done. All I can do is try to fix my mistakes."

"Lying won't do that."

"But telling the truth would start a war. What am I supposed to do?"

"She's right, Duke," Kay spoke up. "If this situation isn't dealt with within the next week or so, thousands of innocent lives might be lost."

"Let me guess, you're also a false ambassador?"

Kay pushed himself off the wall he'd been leaning on, stepping over to join me as he gazed at the duke. "My false identity doesn't negate my good intentions, Duke Gladik." He placed his hand over his heart. "Like you, I have a mission to protect and defend what I hold dear, and I will carry out that mission until the very end—even if it costs me my life."

The duke stood up. "And what about your character? Is *this* how you wish to be remembered? As a fraud?"

Kay folded his arms over his chest. "If we don't stop this war, there won't be many people left *to* remember me. If my good character must die in your eyes, then so be it. There are far more important things in life than a good reputation, Duke, so please understand—"

"I don't *want* to understand you!" the duke interrupted. "In fact, even if I did, I doubt I ever could." He lifted his chin, staring at us with ice in his eyes. "Now, if you'll excuse me, Miss Vel— Amelia, Sir Kay, I'm done discussing this with you."

Duke Gladik turned and stalked over to the front door, opening it and slamming it behind him.

I stared at the door, then closed my eyes, holding my head in my hands as a wave of dizziness washed over me.

"Miss Amelia?"

I opened my eyes. Kay watched me with pursed lips and a slight frown. "What do you plan to do now?"

I shut my eyes again. "I don't know," I mumbled. "Before I left Eldnaire, Kyvir gave me a letter to give to the Ivanyaran leaders. But the thing is, he wrote that letter while thinking Myarna was behind the deaths of the ambassadors. I don't see what good it would do to deliver that message now."

"I agree," Kay said. "I'd say that right now, it's more important that the emperor learns the truth—before the conflict between our countries has a chance to escalate. During our fight in the forest, the archer who shot me managed to escape, so it won't be long before the person who hired the mercenaries learns that the assassination attempt failed. We don't have much time."

I reopened my eyes and turned, looking out the window as a cart rattled down the street past the house. A group of children ran by soon after, and the muffled sound of their laughter reached my ears. I turned back to Kay. "I think...maybe you should go back to Eldnaire without me."

He frowned. "Miss Amelia, you're the one who the emperor appears to trust. If I were to return to Eldnaire without you, he might suspect that I harmed you."

"Duke Gladik would be able to vouch for you."

Kay's frown deepened. "That doesn't mean that he would. There are thousands of lives on the line, Miss Amelia. Your friends, your neighbors, the people who smile or wave at you as you pass by them on the street, the patrons you serve when you work at the library. And, while I'm not certain that simply inform- ing the emperor of his nobles' treachery will be enough to save our country, it's the best—if not the only—option that we have available to us at this point in time."

I looked over at the mantel. Without the family heirlooms, the stone shelf looked lonely and bare—friendless and hopeless. I sighed. "I'm sure everything will work out... Kyvir said he'd do everything in his power to avoid war."

"Even if that's the truth, the emperor's power is limited," Kay argued. "And once the idea of war has been seeded in the minds of the Vilnarian people, no amount of good intentions or naive platitudes will change anything."

"If that's true, then maybe my father was right..." A dry laugh escaped my lips. "Maybe there really is no way to stop the war."

Kay crossed his arms over his chest. "I wasn't implying that you should give up."

I threw my hands up. "Well, maybe I should! I'm not sure if I have any other options left, Kay. Duke Gladik is furious, Leon is injured, and my family is leaving. My father is right. The more I tried to 'fix' things, the worse things became."

Kay stepped closer. "Don't forget what's at stake here, Miss Amelia. You could choose to run away and leave the rest of us to deal with the consequences of your actions, but do you want to live the rest of your life knowing that you could have helped us but didn't?"

I turned my back to him, staring at my boots. "No…but I can't choose Myarna over my family."

"I hope that you'll reconsider your decision, Miss Amelia… before it's too late."

Anger rose to the back of my throat like bile, and I pressed my lips together to keep it from spilling out as I raised my hand to touch the bandages wrapped around my arm. What right did Kay have to judge my decision? We hardly knew each other, and yet, here he was, lecturing me as if I were a child. Why did he care so much about whether I stayed with my family or traveled back to Eldnaire? Kyvir would listen whether or not I went back. He would do whatever it took to achieve peace. He had given me his word.

Kay sighed. "In any case, neither of us are in any shape to travel at the moment. So please, take this time to rest and think. Why don't we meet tomorrow to discuss this more?"

I heaved a sigh of my own, letting out some of my frustration.

"I suppose I can do that much, at least." I glanced over my shoulder. "What about the duke?"

Kay grimaced. "Don't worry about him for now. I can't imagine he'd go running back to Vilnaria to divulge our secrets now that he knows the truth about his fellow nobles. But I'll go and find him to ensure that he doesn't get himself into any trouble."

I turned to face Kay. "All right…in that case, if you need a place to stay tonight, you can get a room at—"

"I'll meet you at noon tomorrow at Wolf's Den Inn," he cut in. "Good day, Miss Amelia."

He turned and crossed the room, opening the front door. The house felt as empty as an upside-down water bucket once he left. I stood in the center of the room, staring at the front door for a while as my thoughts played tug-of-war with my heart. My father's question repeated itself over and over again in my mind. *"Do you love your family?"*

The answer was obvious, but my next steps weren't. Whether I left with my family or went back to Vilnaria with Kay, I'd be leaving everything I once knew behind. The house, the library, everything—and everyone—I grew up with. I'd have to start all over again. Nothing would ever be the same.

I put my hands to my throat as if that would stop my thoughts from suffocating me. The air in the house no longer reached my lungs, and my hands shook. My vision blurred and doubled, showing me two, fuzzy-looking front doors.

My feet moved on their own, propelling me toward the front door. My fingers reached out, grasping the knob and flinging the door open.

Five

 I wandered aimlessly around town, passing shops and narrowly avoiding being run into by purpose-driven pedestrians. When I finally stopped, I found myself outside of a familiar home. It was an old, gray, stone two-story building with a slate roof. Window boxes filled with violas hung beneath the large windows, adding a splash of color to the gray. An ornate stone archway a shade darker than the rest of the house stood over the door. The name "Dourain" had been engraved in the arch's large keystone.

Sadie Dourain and I had been friends since we were seven years old—though I still wasn't quite sure how it happened. Sadie was elegant and confident, bubbly and outgoing—everything I wasn't. Her ancestors had helped found Averndale, and despite their lack of noble titles, the Dourain family was well-respected.

Sadie's mother ran their family's textile business, while her father was the head magistrate's assistant, an important member of the Council of Law—a fact that didn't occur to me until I stood on their doorstep, fist poised to knock at the front door.

Though Sadie was my friend, spending time with someone connected to the Council of Law after impersonating a government official and committing fraud and treason sounded like tempting fate to turn against me...again.

Sadie was bound to ask me where I'd been and what I'd been doing. I had already lied to so many people since traveling to Vilnaria. I didn't want to include Sadie on that list, so the most sensible thing to do would be to walk away.

I lowered my hand to my side, but before I could turn around, the door opened, revealing Sadie herself.

"Lia?"

We stared at each other. My mind sifted through words, trying to find the right ones to say, but nothing came to mind.

Sadie wore a cyan satin gown with black trim around the neckline, waistline, hem, and sleeves. The gown complimented her olive skin and narrow, dark eyes well. Her wavy brown hair had been arranged into a single braid that snaked over her right shoulder, adorned with two faux cyan flowers.

Finally, Sadie let out a laugh and darted forward, throwing her slender arms around me with a squeal. "Lia! I can't believe you're here!"

I hissed in pain as she squeezed my wounded arm in her hug. She pulled back, her hands on top of my shoulders as she searched my face. "Are you all right?"

I forced out a laugh. "Yeah, I'm fine... It was just a really rough trip back here."

Sadie clicked her tongue and stepped back, looking me up and down. "I can tell. You look absolutely horrific. What happened?"

She held up a finger. "Wait, don't answer that. Let's get you cleaned up first. Come on in." Before I could say another word, Sadie grabbed my hand and dragged me into her house.

After spending the night in the forest and sleeping on the ground, I was more than happy to have an opportunity to bathe and wash my hair. And thanks to Sadie's perfumed soaps and scented bath salts, it reminded me of my time in Eldnaire.

At the palace, I had access to all sorts of fancy soaps and hair mixtures. It took me a while to get used to it, but now, only a couple of days after leaving, I missed it. My family was by no means poor, but Sadie and the other extremely wealthy people I had met during my trip lived in a world completely foreign compared to the one I had grown up in.

Once I had finished bathing, I dried my hair, re-wrapped the cut on my upper arm, and changed into the cerulean dress Sadie had left out for me.

By the time I rejoined her in her room, I looked like a noblewoman and smelled like a field of lavender. The hot water and calming scents relieved a lot of the tension from the last few days, but now I braced myself for Sadie's questions.

Sadie grinned and clapped her hands as soon as she spotted me. "That's much better! How do you feel?"

"Pretty wonderful," I admitted. I walked over to a chair and collapsed into it, letting out a deep breath. "Thanks, Sadie…"

Sadie beamed. "What are friends for?" She put her hands down on her bed and leaned forward. "And now that you look more alive… Where were you? Your parents said you were supposed to be back days ago!"

"Well, I—"

Sadie jumped up from her bed. "Oh, wait! Why don't we discuss this somewhere more comfortable? I'm famished and there's this new tea shop that opened up a few days ago that I've been *dying* to visit. They're open till six, and it's only around three thirty now, so we'd have plenty of time." Her brown eyes sparkled like sunlight over a lake. "And I heard they have over fifty-six flavors of tea to choose from!"

A smile slid its way onto my face. "That's a lot of tea…"

"Right? So…" she tilted her head to the side. "Would you like to go pay it a visit?"

I raised an eyebrow. "Do I have to drink all fifty-six tea flavors?"

Sadie hummed, then shook her head. "I'll let you off the hook since you just got back."

I smiled. "In that case, you've got yourself a deal."

Six

*T*he streets of Averndale were filled with mothers, wives, and children on their way to or from the marketplace with last-minute ingredients for their dinners and men driving carts full of hay, produce, or caged chickens.

But compared to the normal hustle and bustle of Eldnaire's fashionable society—with its gilded carriages, curricles, and noisy crowds—Averndale's idea of busyness looked rather peaceful.

As we walked through town, Sadie took it upon herself to catch me up on all the high-society gossip I had missed.

"Since you've been gone, so much has happened! Lina Canden got engaged to Fio Danburn under—well, questionable circumstances. Tabitha Willows disappeared a week ago—"

I frowned. "Disappeared?"

She shrugged. "There's been no ransom note if that's what you're worried about. However, she's not the only one who disappeared." Sadie smirked. "Her father's personal assistant disappeared at exactly the same time. Tabitha was known for rejecting proposals, and I suppose now we know why. My guess is that they've eloped."

"Maybe so."

Sadie and I stopped at the corner of the street as a couple of farmers drove their carts past us. The aroma of freshly baked bread wafted out from the open door of the bakery beside us and I closed my eyes, inhaling the scent.

"Hm, that was odd," Sadie mumbled.

I opened my eyes and turned to look at her. "What's odd?"

Sadie shrugged, nodding to the right, over to the other side of the street. "I thought I saw one of my father's colleagues over there, by the flower shop, so I waved, but he ducked into the alleyway."

My gaze drifted to the alley between the flower and milliner's shop. From my current angle, all I could see was the stark contrast between the late afternoon sunlight—which touched the ground and part of the wall visible from where we stood—and the shadow of the buildings that cast the rest of the alleyway in darkness.

I turned back to Sadie. "Perhaps you were mistaken?"

She frowned. "It's possible… I guess it was a little far away, but he was the right height and build—and I could have sworn I saw a scar on his forehead."

A picture of Kay, with his muscular build and scarred forehead, flashed into my mind. Surely Sadie wasn't talking about Kay. After all, he wasn't on the Council, and what reason would he have to follow us?

And yet, how many other people in Myarna had scars on their foreheads? Was it truly that common?

"Your father's colleague," I began, "what's his name?"

"Benjamin," Sadie smiled. "We've met several times before—he's even joined my family for dinner on a few occasions. He's a true gentleman in every sense of the word, and he's unbelievably handsome."

Benjamin, not Kay. My shoulders relaxed. "I see…"

Sadie flicked her braid behind her shoulder and adjusted the flower in her hair. "That's it, I'm convinced. It must not have been him. If Benjamin *had* seen me, I know he would have come over and greeted us. He's too polite to ignore a lady that he's well-acquainted with."

I smothered a chuckle as the two of us crossed the street, leaving the alley and the man who "couldn't be Benjamin" behind.

"I suppose this Benjamin is your latest admirer?"

"I'm not sure." Sadie glared at the ground as she walked. "I can't tell if he's attracted to me or if he's just being a gentleman, and it's driving me mad!"

I didn't bother restraining my laughter this time as we reached the other side of the street. "Well, this is a first. A man who hasn't proposed to you after your first meeting? No wonder you like him."

Sadie halted and a woman who was walking behind us nearly bumped right into her. Sadie stepped out of the woman's path, eyes wide. "My apologies!"

The woman flashed her a smile and continued striding down the path.

Sadie and I walked forward again, and she glared at me. "I never said that I *liked* Benjamin. It just infuriates me when men hide their true intentions—that's all," she huffed. Her eyes lit up. "Oh, I didn't finish telling you my news."

"There's…more?"

Sadie nodded. "I told you about Lina and Tabitha, but that's not even the most shocking thing that's happened during the last couple of weeks!" She glanced around, then lowered her voice, leaning closer to me. "Just two nights ago, young Lord Mackaby was caught drinking and gambling at a tavern in the rough part of town—on the same night that the guards were called there to break up a brawl. And rumor has it that *he* started it—though no one knows why."

"His parents must be furious."

Sadie stopped in her tracks, gawking at me. "Furious? They were absolutely enraged! Especially since it led to his fiancée calling off their engagement—and just three weeks before the wedding!"

I nodded and hummed out a response as we started walking again. I had never been too interested in the lives of people that I'd likely never meet, but Sadie *lived* for scandals and rumors—and the more scandalous the rumor, the better.

After being involved in such a large scandal of my own, I couldn't help but feel a twinge of empathy for the subjects of Sadie's gossip. How many of the rumors were actually true? How much about them had been fabricated? What if things simply spiraled out of control as they had for Leon and me?

In all likelihood, the true story would never be told. Nobody would ever know what really happened. Nobody but those involved.

"Oh, and speaking of scandals, what was it like in Vilnaria?" Sadie eyed me. "I know you're not the type to seek out gossip, and since you were just there to deliver books I suppose you didn't run into any Vilnarian royals, but tell me…are the people there as rude and muleheaded as they say?"

I frowned. "Uh, no… At least, none of the Vilnarians that *I* met were particularly rude. I did meet a few that were rather stubborn, though—" As I spoke, I spotted Duke Gladik himself across the street, talking to two menacing, burly men. My breath caught in my throat. Didn't Kay say that he would find the duke and make sure he didn't get into any trouble? Myarna was large, but surely Kay would have little problem finding someone who stood out as much as the duke did, with his blond hair and green riding suit. It had been at least two hours since Kay left my house, so why wasn't he with the duke? Unless…the man Sadie had seen in the alley and mistook for her father's colleague had actually been *Kay*.

One of the men took a step closer to the duke and I shook those speculations out of my mind, turning to look at Sadie. "Sadie, I—there's something I need to do. I'll be right back!"

Before she could respond, I dashed forward, dodging past a horse and cart carrying hay, and crossed to the other side of the street. As I approached the duke, one of the men speaking with him—a tall, broad-shouldered man with short, spiky black hair—crossed his arms. "We did you a service, didn't we? The least you could do is make it worth our while, *foreigner*," he said.

Duke Gladik shook his head. "An entire gold coin seems quite excessive. I merely asked you for a simple favor."

The other thug snorted. "Ya rich folk are'll the same… Ya 'ave a lot, but can't be bother'd to share none of it."

The duke's eyes narrowed. "I am more than happy to compensate anyone for their time and energy…as long as the compensation is proportionate to the service rendered."

The two men looked at each other. The spiky-haired one shrugged, and they both turned back to Duke Gladik.

"Jus' hand yer coin purse ov'r," the short, stocky thug growled.

I stepped forward. "Mr. Gladik! I've been looking everywhere for you!"

Duke Gladik turned. His eyes widened upon seeing me. "Miss Amelia?"

I flashed a smile at him. "Why don't I show you around Averndale? It can be a little confusing if you aren't familiar with the area."

The spiky-haired thug glared at me. "And who are *you?*"

"This man's guide." I turned to the duke. "Shall we go now?"

"Yer not going anywhere till ya give us whatever ya got," the short thug snarled.

I looked around, but Sadie was nowhere in sight. Due to the approaching dinner hour, the crowd had thinned out in this part of town, and those who were still walking averted their gazes from the trouble brewing on the street corner.

"I won't be giving you *anything.*" Duke Gladik lifted his chin. "And unless you'd like me to contact the authorities, I suggest you let us go now."

"It's two against one." The spiky-haired thug sneered. "I'd say that our odds are better than yers."

I frowned. "He's…he's not alone."

Spiky hair smirked. "He may as well be."

The man could have stabbed me and his words still would

have hurt more. My mind flashed to the forest. Leon, fighting to protect me while I just watched.

A "*shing*" brought me back to the present. Duke Gladik had a sword grasped in his hands. His eyebrows knit together as his blue eyes scrutinized the thugs. "I've tried to be patient with you, but you've gone too far and have shown us both great disrespect. Please, leave now."

The short thug glared at the duke. "Why you—"

The spiky-haired thug grabbed the other guy's shoulder. "Hey, Van, we gotta get out of 'ere. The guards are coming."

The short thug's eyes widened. "What?"

I turned. Sure enough, a group of guards were marching this way, accompanied by Sadie.

"Ya gotta be kiddin' me…" Van glared at the duke. "Ya got lucky ya gold grubb'r!"

The two men turned and ran as the guards dashed after them. "Hey! Stop!" one of the guards called.

Sadie joined Duke Gladik and me, placing her hands on top of my shoulders as she searched my face. "Amelia, are you all right?"

I smiled. "I'm fine… That could have gotten really out of hand…"

Sadie frowned, removing her hands from my shoulders and placing them on her hips. "Yeah. I have to say I was shocked when you ran off with hardly a word." She glanced between Duke Gladik and I. "I take it that the two of you know each other?"

I glanced at the duke. "Oh, yes…we met in Vilnaria."

Sadie blinked. "Then…you're Vilnarian?"

Duke Gladik bowed. "Yes, Miss, I am."

Sadie grinned. "Oh, *and* polite, I see… In that case, Amelia and I were just about to visit a new tea shop. Why don't you join us? Perhaps you and Amelia could tell me a little more about Vilnaria over tea and scones."

Duke Gladik's cheeks reddened as he smiled back. "After the time I've just had, tea sounds lovely…"

The tea shop, Tina's Tea & Pastries, was nestled between an apothecary and a bookshop. Upon entering, I inhaled a myriad of herbal and spicy scents. I recognized peppermint, cinnamon, vanilla, and a citrus of some sort.

Despite how small it appeared from the outside, the interior of the shop was quite spacious. Six tables sat on either side of the aisle leading from the front door to the counter. Each of the chairs and tables were varnished white. Fluffy red cushions lay on the seats of the chairs, and small porcelain vases with red and pink roses sat in the center of each table.

After placing our orders with the staff at the counter, we found a table in the left corner of the store, in front of the shop's large window—on the opposite side of the only other three customers in the shop.

"I'd like to thank you both for your help," Duke Gladik said as we sat down at the table. "I'm not certain I could have resolved that issue peacefully if I were by myself."

Sadie grinned. "No need to thank me! If you're a friend of Lia's, you're a friend of mine." She looked at me. "The two of you *are* friends, right?"

I tapped my fingernails against the table. "It's...a little complicated..."

Sadie frowned. "What's that supposed to mean?"

"I haven't known Miss Amelia for very long, and when I first met her, she wasn't herself." The duke gave me a pointed look.

I winced. "That's true... I was under a lot of stress the first time we met."

"Ah," Sadie tilted her head. "What did Leon do this time?"

Duke Gladik blinked at Sadie. "How did you know Miss Amelia's brother was involved?"

Sadie shrugged. "I've known the two of them for long enough. Lia's always trying to keep him out of trouble."

"And failing miserably," I sighed.

"You wouldn't fail if you quit taking on that job," Sadie said.

I groaned as I placed my arms on the table and rested my head on them. "It's not that simple, Sadie..."

"It sounds pretty simple to me. Tell your brother to look after himself. Let him face the consequences of his own actions for once."

I sighed into my arms before sitting up. "If only you had said that a week ago."

"So what I'm hearing is, my advice is good, I just have to work on my timing." Sadie hummed. "Good to know."

I raised an eyebrow. "Oh?"

Sadie let out a laugh. "Oh yeah...I guess that's another thing I haven't been able to tell you yet." She grinned. "I've been thinking about following in my father's footsteps."

My eyes widened. "You're going to join the Council of Law?"

Sadie leaned forward and reached out, rearranging the roses in the vase. "I mean, it's either that or continue helping my mother with the textile business... But I think I'd like to try out the law."

Duke Gladik studied Sadie. "Is your father truly on Myarna's Council of Law?"

Sadie sat back with a grin. "He's the only one who can argue with the head magistrate *and* get away with it."

"Mr. Dourain certainly has a way with words," I agreed. "He could talk a snail into giving up its shell."

Duke Gladik's lips turned up. "He sounds like quite the interesting man."

"He is—oh!" I gasped, meeting the duke's blue eyes. "I was wondering...have you seen Kay?"

The duke's smile slid from his face. "No, not since I left your house. Why do you ask?"

My tongue froze within my mouth. Was it true, then? Had Kay been following Sadie and me? And if so, why? What was he trying to do?

"Miss Amelia? Is everything all right?"

The duke's words snapped me from my thoughts and unthawed my tongue. "I certainly hope so." I forced a smile as a server walked toward our table, carrying a tray with all our orders balanced on top.

All I knew at the moment was that Sadie thought she saw a man with a scar on his forehead duck into an alleyway, and the duke hadn't seen Kay since earlier in the afternoon. I had no proof that Kay was up to anything sinister. He had helped take out the mercenaries in the forest, and his loyalty appeared to lie with Myarna—not Vilnaria. Besides, making assumptions without any evidence was what led me into trouble in the first place. I would just have to trust Kay…at least for now.

Seven

After receiving our tea and pastries, Sadie looked between Duke Gladik and me. "All right, I think I've waited long enough. Tell me everything about Vilnaria. What's it like?"

"It's a lot busier than Averndale." The duke picked up his teacup. "At least in the capital—where I live. In recent years, new holidays and festivals have been added to the calendar, so there's almost always something to celebrate or a reason to host another ball—"

Sadie perked up. "Do you attend balls often?"

The duke nodded. "Yes, I do. I enjoy dancing, and they often serve chocolate plum cake—which happens to be my favorite dessert."

Sadie placed a finger to her chin, tilting her head to the side as she studied the duke. "Excuse me if I'm being a little too nosy, but I just have to ask... Are you a noble?"

I set my teacup and saucer down on the table. "Oh, right, I suppose we never did get around to introductions." I looked toward the duke. "Sadie, allow me to introduce you to Duke Gladik."

Sadie's jaw dropped. "You're a duke? Like, an actual, title-and-land duke?"

"Yes, that's correct." The duke took a sip of his tea.

Sadie whipped around to look at me. "Amelia, I thought you said you didn't meet any royals!"

"I never said that..." I picked up my teacup and saucer. "You assumed that I didn't, and I never had a chance to correct you because you changed the subject."

Sadie blinked, then laughed. "Well, now I *have* to know how the two of you met. Seriously Lia, how did you, of all people, ever manage to befriend a duke?"

I cleared my throat. "That's a...very long story, and I should probably be getting back home soon... My parents will be wondering where I am."

Sadie narrowed her eyes. "You can't get out of it that easily—you haven't even finished your tea yet. Come on, Lia. What happened?"

I squirmed under Sadie's piercing gaze. "Well...Leon and I met the duke at a ball—"

Sadie slammed both hands down on the table with a bang. The table shook, and Sadie's teacup rattled. The milky liquid sloshed over the golden rim and dribbled down to the saucer. "You actually attended a *ball*?"

"It's not what you think," I said, glancing around the teashop. Two out of the three customers stared at us from across the room. I quickly turned back to Sadie. "The truth is, Leon and I weren't even supposed to be there..."

Sadie's eyes widened. She leaned back in her chair, slapping a hand over her mouth. Dropping her hand, she lowered her voice. "The two of you snuck into the royal palace and attended a ball?"

I blinked. "What? No!" I placed my cup down and frowned. "I mean…sort of, but it wasn't like that."

Sadie's eyes gleamed. "Well, did you get to dance?"

My thoughts flashed to the emperor and the first dance we had shared, and how nervous I had been. The way he had smiled and reassured me. "Yes… Yes, I did dance."

Sadie raised an eyebrow. "You're smiling. Was he handsome?"

Heat shot to my cheeks. "What? Was I smiling?"

Sadie giggled. "I'll take that as a yes then." She shook her head. "So you and Leon snuck into the ballroom, and you got swept away by a handsome noble… No wonder it took you so long to return home."

"Sadie, you really have the wrong idea." I sighed.

Sadie eyed me. "Do I?"

I opened my mouth, then closed it. Sadie wasn't completely wrong. Leon and I had been let into the palace on false pretenses, and Kyvir was certainly handsome. My cheeks grew warm at the thought of his hazel eyes and bright smile, and I lowered my head.

"Maybe instead of joining the Council of Law, you should become a novelist," I grumbled into my teacup. "You've managed to make a simple mistake sound like the plot of a romance novel."

Sadie crossed her arms. "Well, unless you tell me how I'm wrong, I'll just have to assume that I'm correct." She gasped. "Wait…Duke Gladik, are *you* the one who swept Amelia off her feet?"

The duke froze. His cheeks were cardinal red—likely as red

as mine—and his eyes grew wide as he stared at Sadie. "Me? I—no! No, I haven't had the pleasure of dancing with Miss Amelia."

Sadie's smile dropped. "Is that so?" She turned back to me. "Then who *did* you dance with?"

I fixed my gaze on the roses in the center of the table. "Does it really matter?"

"Is that a serious question?"

"My…tea is getting cold." I picked up my teacup, bringing it to my lips.

"Lia!" Sadie glared.

I gulped down my lukewarm tea before setting the cup back on the table. I looked up at Sadie. "Leon danced, too."

Sadie's glare slipped from her face, replaced by shock. "What? With who?"

"Most of the ladies there, I'd say."

Sadie frowned. "He didn't dance at the ball I invited you both to…"

"Sadie, his leg was broken."

"Ah, right." She sighed. "He really picked the perfect time to go and break his leg, didn't he?"

I shook my head but couldn't stop the corners of my mouth from turning into a smile. My diversion had worked better than expected. "Well, if it makes you feel any better, Leon wasn't exactly thrilled about his condition either."

Sadie glared at her strawberry scone. "If he would stop being so reckless then maybe he wouldn't get into so many accidents."

I frowned. As we spoke, Leon lay in bed with a long gash across his chest. A wound he'd gotten not from climbing a tree, or attempting to ride an angry bull, but from trying to protect me. I did nothing but jump around like a frightened rabbit during the attack, and if it weren't for Duke Gladik, Leon and I might've both died by that mercenary's hands.

"Lia? Are you listening?"

My gaze snapped up to meet Sadie's. "Oh, sorry…I was just thinking."

"About what?"

I shook my head. "It's not important." I stood. "I should go."

Sadie's face fell. "Is something wrong?"

I flashed a smile. "No, it's just—I left the house without letting my parents know. They might think that I ran off again and worry if I don't come back soon. And besides, I have to help Duke Gladik."

Sadie frowned. "You still haven't told me very much about Vilnaria, or why your trip back was so rough."

"I'll tell you whatever you want to know the next time we meet," I promised.

"And when will that be?"

"I'm not sure…but it'll happen."

Her frown deepened. "Amelia, now you're worrying me."

"I'm sorry, Sadie…" I looked at the duke, who was swallowing the last bite of his scone. "Duke Gladik, will you please escort me home? I can give you some directions on the way."

The duke nodded, standing. "Of course." He turned and bowed to Sadie. "It was lovely meeting you, Miss Sadie. And thank you again for your help earlier."

Sadie grimaced. "Yes…it was nice meeting you, too."

"Your friend was very kind," Duke Gladik spoke as we walked down the street. The sun had begun setting and painted the sky with pinks, oranges, and a hint of periwinkle.

I nodded, walking fast to keep up with the duke. "She is… I'm truly grateful for her friendship."

The duke frowned. "Then why didn't you tell her the truth? You didn't even inform her about Leon's injury."

"Her father is on the Council of Law, and he'd be obligated to report anything he heard," I explained. "It wouldn't be fair to tell her everything that happened in Vilnaria and then expect her not to tell her father."

"So, you won't tell her because you're afraid of the consequences," the duke huffed.

I pursed my lips. My boot hit a loose stone, kicking it down the street. "Of course I'm afraid. Leon and I could be executed." As the words left my mouth, a shiver rattled up my spine. At least the Council of Law was currently unaware of the crimes my brother and I committed. Duke Gladik, on the other hand, knew everything. He held our lives in his hands. One word from him, and we'd be heading straight for the gallows—especially if Leon or I ever did go back to Vilnaria.

"It's just as I said before. Lies get people killed."

I glared at the duke. "You act like you've never made a single mistake in your entire life, Duke Gladik."

"I've made plenty of mistakes, Miss Amelia, and all of them have had consequences that I didn't want to face."

"Well, I haven't," I snapped.

The duke stopped walking. "Excuse me?"

I looked up at him, guilt and frustration burning within me. "I'm not the one who makes mistakes. *Leon* makes mistakes—a lot of mistakes. And I'm the one who fixes them. That's how it's always been—how I thought it always would be. But the one time *I* make a mistake, I single-handedly manage to bring two countries to the brink of war—"

I froze, mid-rant, as I spotted a woman carrying a basket down the street walking toward us. I glanced at her as she passed, but her gaze was fixed on her basket.

Once she had walked farther down the street, the duke spoke again. "I think you're giving yourself too much credit, Miss Amelia. The cart was already rolling down the hill when you pushed it."

"Perhaps..." I murmured. "But maybe things would have turned out better if I'd never gotten involved."

"No, we'd already be at war."

I stared at the duke. "What do you mean?"

Duke Gladik sighed. "If you and Leon hadn't stepped in, my fellow nobles would have been able to use their plan to frame Myarna for the deaths of the Ivanyaran ambassadors. They would have used the incident to pressure the emperor into declaring war. What you and your brother did was foolish, criminal, and despicable, but I have to admit, it did postpone the bloodshed."

I stared up at the sky above. A couple of clouds dotted the expanse, tinged with the hues of sunset. He was right. By taking the place of the ambassadors, we had delayed the war—even if we hadn't managed to stop it completely. I lowered my gaze to the duke.

"You…really thought about this, didn't you."

He nodded and started walking again, slower. "Of course I have." He glanced at me. "This is a serious situation, Miss Amelia. I don't know who I can trust back in Eldnaire, so I'll have to decide on my next course of action now, before I return."

"Do you have any ideas yet?" I asked as we approached my house.

"A few…but nothing concrete."

I grimaced. "Well, Kay and I are supposed to meet at Wolf's Den Inn tomorrow at noon to discuss our next steps. Would you join us?"

"I don't trust either of you completely. But at least you're more trustworthy than my fellow nobles." The duke narrowed his eyes. "I'll join both of you tomorrow, but I won't be making any promises to cooperate."

Despite the hint of bitterness in his tone, the duke's words filled me with relief. I stopped as we approached the street my house was on, turning to the duke. "I understand. And…thank you."

He frowned. "For what?"

"You've helped me make my decision." I looked up at the multicolored sky and let out a deep breath. "I won't be returning to Eldnaire."

"What?"

I flashed a smile at the duke. "I think it's time for me to step back. I'll write a letter to Kyvir, and you and Kay can tell him the truth about the nobles. There's no reason for me to involve myself any further."

Duke Gladik stared. "Miss Amelia, don't you think that you're being a bit...rash?"

I shrugged. "Wouldn't it be even more rash to abandon my family and run back to Vilnaria? The war has to be stopped before it even starts—that is important. But there's no reason for all three of us to return to Eldnaire right now."

The duke frowned. "But I...I thought that you and the emperor cared for each other. Or was that also a lie?"

My gaze dropped to the cracked stone sett street. "It's... not a lie. At least, not on my part..." My hand reached up, grasping my necklace. "But I...I don't want to make things worse again—not just between Myarna, Ivanyar, and Vilnaria—but my family. You saw how worried and upset my mother and father were. Leon and I are their only children. We've avoided murder attempts, the law, and execution, but how long is that luck going to last? If something happens to us, then my parents will..."

Duke Gladik placed a hand on my shoulder. "I understand."

I looked up. "You do?"

"Yes." The duke gave me a sad smile. "My father used to say that his allegiance would forever and always be to his family first, his subordinates second, and his country third." He removed his hand and turned, looking at the neighborhood. "He said that countries and cultures change over time, empires rise and fall, and rulers may easily be replaced—but those we love cannot."

"Your father sounds like a wonderful man," I murmured.

"He was." Duke Gladik glanced at me. "I envy you, Miss Amelia."

I blinked. "What? Why?"

"Because you have the option to put your family first. I have to settle for my subordinates."

Kyvir had said that Duke Gladik was the youngest duke in the empire, but only now did I realize why the duke had inherited the title early. Without his parents around, the duke must have had to step up and fill their places. Unexpectedly, my heart ached for the duke. His eyes spoke of pain and loneliness. Loss that could never be recovered.

I lowered my voice. "Then…do you think I'm making the right choice?"

The duke looked at me. His blue eyes shone. "I do."

I let out a deep breath. "Then I'll just have to convince Kay of that tomorrow."

The duke nodded. "Do you think you'll ever return to Eldnaire?"

"Of course… I made Kyvir a promise that I don't plan on breaking." I looked up. By now, the sun had dropped to the line of rooftops. "Even if it takes some time, I'll keep my promise and fix my mistakes…no matter what."

After giving Duke Gladik directions to Wolf's Den Inn, we parted ways. On the street in front of my house sat a black carriage with a red, shield-shaped crest on the side. A silver sword had been painted onto the crest, dividing it vertically straight down the middle. Green ivy had been painted onto the sword, and wrapped loosely around the hilt and the length of the blade.

I'd seen both the carriage and the crest plenty of times. All members of the Council of Law used the black, crested carriages—including Sadie's father. As I passed by, the driver stared at me like I had just kicked his horse.

I averted my gaze and hurried up the walkway to the front door. Upon entering my home, my eyes immediately landed on my parents. They sat on the couch, lips drawn into thin lines. My mother's eyes were red, and her hands remained in her lap, clasped so tight that her knuckles were white. My father had his arm around her. His gaze fixed on his brown polished shoes.

Two chairs from the table near the mantel had been turned around, and two well-dressed men sat in them. And next to the man on the left stood Kay.

I stopped in my tracks, looking between them. "What's...going on? Is something wrong? Is it Leon?"

"The only one you should be worrying about right now is yourself," one of the men said, standing up. "Amelia Huld, you are under arrest for high treason."

Eight

*A*n hour later, I found myself sitting in the middle of a small room with white walls, across the table from the Council's interrogator.

The Council's red crest had been painted on the wall in front of me, and above it, the words "Hall of Truth." False torches were fixed on either side of the crest on the wall. Instead of fire, light crystals lit up the room, bright and unwavering.

In the corner of the room behind me, I heard the scuffling of chairs, and a man coughed. I didn't dare look to see how many people were watching, but I knew that Kay had to be one of them. Kay had half-dragged me from the carriage to the accusations office without a word, and I didn't bother asking him what he was doing. It was clear now that Kay was never truly on our side.

"Answer the question!"

My chains jangled as I jumped in my seat, snapping out of my thoughts as the interrogator growled at me. He was a tall, thin man with small, dark eyes, bushy eyebrows, a balding head, and a perpetual scowl.

"I—" I coughed on my dry words. "I'm sorry... What did you say?"

"Who do you work for?" the man growled.

"I...I'm a librarian... I work for my parents, Aiden and Vya Huld—" I yelped, shrinking back into my seat as the man slammed his fist down on the wooden table.

"Answer the question!" he roared. "Who do you work for?"

"I'm telling you the truth! I work for my parents here in town as a librarian!" I cried.

"Then tell me what you and your brother were doing in Vilnaria."

I swallowed hard. My body shook. "We were there to deliver some books that were borrowed from the imperial library."

"Are books all that you delivered?"

"Yes—well, no...we never ended up delivering the books to the imperial library ourselves—someone else did that."

"Who?" The interrogator glowered.

My stomach flopped. "I don't know...all I was told was that someone would ensure that the books were safely delivered for us."

The man placed both of his palms on the table, leaning forward. "And who told you that?"

"Sir Fern," I said.

"And who is Sir Fern?"

"Sir Richard Ferdinand Isaacs, of Vilnaria."

The interrogator narrowed his eyes. "The Vilnarian emperor's adviser?"

I nodded. "That's right."

"And why would a Myarnan librarian have anything to do with the adviser of a foreign country?"

"Because…" I stopped. If I continued talking, there'd be no going back. The words could never be unsaid. My guilt would be set in stone—and not just mine. Leon and I would both suffer.

"Because?" The interrogator prompted.

I was done with all the lies. All the hiding. Duke Gladik was right. Lies kill people. So did the truth, but even so, it needed to be said.

I let out a deep breath and opened my mouth, looking up at the scowling man. "Because I made a mistake…a lot of them."

The interrogator leaned back in his wooden chair. "Do tell— and don't leave anything out."

Once I finished telling the interrogator all the details of my stay in Vilnaria, he sat back, staring at me. At some point during my explanation, his scowl had slipped from his face, replaced with a grimace.

"And you really expect me to believe a story this far-fetched?"

I stared down at my chained wrists. "No, sir…I don't. But it's the truth. It was never my intention to betray my country…I simply wanted to do the right thing."

"At the expense of the lives of your fellow countrymen?"

I shut my eyes, lowering my head. "I…I didn't realize I was

putting them in danger until a few days ago."

"Tell me, Miss Huld. How many people do you think we've executed for high treason in the past?"

I opened my eyes, looking up at the man. "I don't... I don't know, sir."

"Then I'll tell you." He leaned forward. "*None*. You and your brother would be the first."

I swallowed hard. My chains clanked together as I clenched my fists to my heart.

The officer looked past me, over my shoulder. "Is that enough information for all of you?"

I followed his gaze, turning my head. Now I could see four people sitting in chairs against the wall behind me. Kay, the two men who had been at my house when I was arrested, and a woman.

One of the men nodded, standing. He wore a long, black robe over a white collared shirt. His thin, long gray hair had been tied back, and he wore a pair of spectacles on his nose. "I'm still not sure what to make of the story, but yes, I think we've heard enough." He glanced at Kay. "Benjamin, does this woman's story line up with everything you've learned?"

My mouth dropped open. *Benjamin? Kay was Sadie's "Benjamin" after all.*

Kay gave a nod. "Yes, odd as her story is, it appears to be the truth."

"Then I'd say we're all in quite the predicament." He turned to look at me. "Miss Huld, I'm guessing that, by now, you know the gravity of the situation. You must understand what will happen should our country be blamed for sabotaging relations between Ivanyar and Vilnaria."

I lowered my head, staring at my hands in my lap. "Yes...I understand."

"Then you will stay here in Averndale's law office until we come up with an appropriate sentence."

I looked up. "I won't be given a trial?"

The older man shook his head. "Due to the sensitive and urgent nature of this case, no, I'm afraid we won't be able to grant you that right."

I slumped farther down in my seat. "Oh..."

The man turned to Kay. "Benjamin, please escort Miss Huld to cell number—"

The man was interrupted by a knock at the door. A young woman entered, walking up to the man and whispering something in his ear.

He raised an eyebrow and nodded. "I see. Thank you, Eliza." He looked to Kay. "Benjamin, please escort Amelia back to her residence. She is to be placed on house arrest until further notice."

Kay stood. "Yes, sir."

"Wait, Head Magistrate, I must protest!" The other man—a younger man wearing a brown robe with a pinched face—shot to his feet. "House arrest? For a high treasonist? Sir, you must think of the precedent you're setting."

The head magistrate turned his gaze to the man. "Amelia Huld has not been officially sentenced yet, and her brother is already under house arrest due to his injuries. Neither of them are currently considered flight risks, and this is Amelia's first known offense."

"Still—"

The head magistrate's eyes narrowed. "Lord Henley."

Lord Henley bowed his head. "My apologies, Head Magistrate…"

The head magistrate turned back to Kay. "Please continue, Benjamin. And return as soon as you can." He glanced at me, then at the other Council members. "We have much to discuss."

I wasn't sure just how long I had spent inside the accusations office, but the sky had turned to ink by the time I left Averndale's Council of Law. Kay led me to another black, red-crested carriage. After giving the driver the directions, he helped me into the carriage then sat across from me.

The carriage jerked forward, and I braced myself to keep from tumbling straight into Kay. Regaining my balance, I leaned back against the red cushioned interior of the carriage. Light from the crystal street lamps shone through the windows into the carriage at short intervals, lighting up Kay's face for brief moments.

I looked at him, my shoulders tensed. "So…your name isn't Kay?"

"No, but you can keep calling me by that name."

I frowned. "Who exactly are you?"

"My real name is Benjamin," Kay said. "I work for the Council of Law."

My frown deepened. That much was clear. But if Kay had ended up in Vilnaria, and knew someone as important as Sir Fern, then he couldn't be an ordinary member of the Council. "Are you a spy?"

He looked out the window. "The less you know, the better."

I clutched my necklace. "In all likelihood, I'm about to be executed. So I'd be taking your secrets to my grave," I murmured.

Kay glanced at me. "I apologize for informing my superiors about you and your brother. I'm sure you were shocked to find out that I'm not who I claimed to be."

I stared at him. "Shocked? I truly thought that you asked to come along on our journey because you wanted to help us *fix* this mess… But it turns out that you just wanted to send us to the gallows! Of course, I'm shocked!" I shut my eyes. "I can't believe I didn't realize anything strange about you earlier. You knew so much about the duke, the imperial family, and Vilnaria's affairs— but I can't recall a single detail you've given us about yourself."

"Gathering intelligence is a large part of my job," Kay said. "Sharing my personal affairs is not."

The carriage continued clattering down the stone sett street. My toes curled over in my boots. "What will happen to my parents?"

"Did they have anything to do with your crimes?"

I opened my eyes and quickly shook my head. "No, they didn't even know where we were."

"Then they'll be fine."

I looked out the window, watching the crystal street lamps as we passed them. A few minutes later, the carriage rolled to a stop.

"Here we are," Kay announced. "A few guards are already posted around the area, so don't leave your house." He turned to look at me. "If they think you're trying to escape, things will only get worse for you and your family."

"I understand." I pursed my lips. Through the carriage window, I could see the silhouette of my house. Light shone from the front room, which meant my parents were still awake.

The thought of facing them after being arrested and dragged down to the law office turned my stomach.

Kay helped me down from the carriage and escorted me to the door. "Goodbye, Miss Amelia," he said.

I turned my back on him. "Bye, Kay."

I opened the front door of my house and stepped inside. I had scarcely closed the front door behind me when my mother's arms wrapped around my waist. She buried her face in my shoulder, sobbing into it. Standing there, held in my mother's arms, my vision blurred. And all the fear, panic, guilt, and regret I had bottled up poured out through my tears.

My mother flitted back and forth between checking on Leon and crying over me. Father wouldn't look at me, let alone speak to me. He spent his time holed away in his office, hunched over his desk, writing.

My mother finally cried herself to sleep while sitting next to me on the brown leather couch. Despite the late hour, I was wide awake. I got up—careful to avoid waking my mother—and tip-toed into the hallway, slipping into Leon's room.

His room looked just as I remembered it. Light-green wallpaper with white, swirling designs, a desk beneath the singular window in his room, a large old wardrobe in the right corner farthest from the door, and a chest of drawers on the wall next to it. The chair that usually sat at his desk had been dragged over to his bed—likely by Mother. The small, light crystal lamp on his bedside table had been covered with a heavy lampshade, so it cast a dim, warm light on its surroundings—including Leon. He was propped up by pillows and lifted his gaze to mine as I entered. "Oh, hey Lia."

I froze. "Leon?"

He grinned. "Why'd you sound so surprised? You didn't think I was actually dying, did you?"

At the mention of dying, the inevitable verdict clawed at my thoughts, and tears sprang to my eyes. "Leon, I'm so sorry…"

Leon frowned. "Hey, what's wrong?"

I stepped over and sat down on the chair by his bed. "It's…it's the Council of Law."

"Oh, right…Father did mention something about that during his last lecture. They visited our house for something, right?"

"They know everything." I shuddered. "They're probably discussing our sentence as we speak."

Leon's eyes flickered in surprise, but he smiled. "Hey, don't worry 'bout it, Lia. Sadie's father is on the Council, right? So during our trial, I'm sure that he'll—"

"We're not getting a trial."

Leon blinked. "What?"

I swallowed hard. "They said that they want to keep this information from the public to avoid causing mass panic, so we won't be getting a trial."

Leon tried to sit up but let out a muffled cry of pain, laying back against the pillows.

My eyes widened. "Leon, are you all right?"

Leon's fists clenched. He glared at the ceiling. "No trial? That's—how could they do that? It's completely unlawful!"

My shoulders relaxed. "I think it's a little too late for us to start caring about the law now, Leon…"

Leon pressed his lips together, his face growing pale. "I'm being serious, Amelia. They can't do this. If we don't get a trial, we shouldn't get a sentence either—why did you tell them everything? They never would have known if you hadn't—"

"Kay was a spy for the Council," I interrupted. "*He's* the one who informed them about us posing as ambassadors, and *then* I got arrested for high treason. They already knew everything before they interrogated me."

Leon stared at me. "You're joking…"

I shook my head. "He's been planning to turn us in since we left Eldnaire."

He blinked. "Oh."

"I'm so sorry…" I murmured.

Leon stared up at the ceiling, swallowing hard. "Do you really think they'll execute us?"

I closed my eyes, leaning back in the chair. "What else would they do?"

"I don't know… Lock us away for the rest of our lives or something, I guess."

I winced. "That's almost just as bad, isn't it?"

"Yeah."

A wave of exhaustion washed over my body, and I allowed my arms to go limp. If I died or spent the rest of my life in a prison cell, would Kyvir wonder what became of me? Would he try to find out, or would he move on with his life as if I had never been a part of it? If only I could see him one last time.

"Lia?"

I opened my eyes, sitting up. "Hm?"

Leon looked at me with tears in his eyes. His jaw trembled. "I'm sorry," he whispered. "Maybe I deserve to die…but you don't."

I gaped at my brother. "Leon…"

He looked away. "I…messed up."

A tear rolled down his cheek and clung to the bottom of his chin. I reached out and placed my hand over his on the bed. "We both messed up, Leon," I whispered. "We both really messed up…"

Nine

*T*he next morning, the head magistrate, Kay, Sadie's father, Lord Henley, and the Councilwoman from the night before arrived at our house. My mother welcomed and showed them into Leon's room since he was still confined to his bed per Dr. Kander's orders.

My father grabbed chairs from all over the house, and the nine of us all managed to find space. I sat in the chair by Leon's bedside, turning it around to face the Council members.

Once we all settled in our seats, the head magistrate cleared his throat and spoke up. "As all of you know, this case is extremely abnormal. As a result, we've had to forgo a public trial and sentencing…"

My heart pounded in my chest, drowning out the head magistrate's opening speech. It didn't feel real. None of it did. Traveling to Vilnaria, meeting Kyvir, getting attacked by mercenaries, Kay being a spy—it all sounded like one of Sadie's stories. I wished it was. I wished it had never happened. My hand crept up to my neck, grabbing hold of my necklace.

No. I was glad that I met Kyvir. But this wasn't how I wanted our story to end.

The head magistrate met my gaze and I froze, sitting up straight in my chair. "In conclusion," he said, "the Council of Law finds Amelia and Leon Huld guilty of high treason and fraud."

His words hung in the air as if they had no other place to go. I had anticipated this verdict all night—thought about how I'd feel and how I'd react. But now that it had been said, I just felt empty. I had no words and no tears left to shed. I lowered my head.

"The sentence for committing treason has always been death," the head magistrate continued, "however, due to the circumstances, the Council has decided to offer you a different option."

I looked up.

"A different option?" my father spoke up, his eyes fixed on the head magistrate. "What is it? What is this different option?"

The head magistrate peered at me from behind his glasses. "Amelia, for some time now, Myarna has been on the precipice of war. A war that our country cannot win. That being the case, the Council is willing to overlook you and your brother's crimes—if you are able to reverse the course we're currently on."

I lowered my brow as the head magistrate's words registered in my brain. "You...want me to stop the war?"

He gave a nod. "If you succeed, I will pardon you and your brother, and the charges against you will all be dropped—as if this whole debacle never happened."

"And if she doesn't succeed?" my father asked. His shoulders were tense, and he sat on the edge of his seat.

The head magistrate looked back in his direction. "In that case, we all lose, don't we?"

"I'll do it," I promised. "I'll do whatever it takes to stop the war."

The magistrate glanced at me. "I suspected as much." He swept his hand out to the side toward Kay. "Very well. Our associate, Benjamin, will accompany you to observe your progress. And, until you return with news of your success, your family will remain under the Council's care." He smiled at me. "So I know you'll do your best."

I stiffened. The magistrate's smile didn't hide the threat behind his words.

My parents' faces turned pale, and my mother placed a hand over her mouth.

"Then…you intend to hold us hostage?" my father asked.

"If the rest of us can't pack up our bags and abandon our country, why should you be able to?" Lord Henley sneered.

"It's all right. I'll return as soon as I can, Father," I said before my father could respond. "I know that Emperor Kyvir will listen to me." I looked around at each person in front of me. "The war won't happen."

"I'll go with you," Leon said from behind me.

"Absolutely not!" Mother and Father snapped in unison.

"You're in no shape to do anything but lie in bed for the next week at least," Mother added.

Leon frowned, then cast a glare in Kay's direction. "Then what, you want her to go with the man who just sold her out?"

"It's fine, Leon," I said. "I'll make this work." I lifted my chin and turned to the head magistrate. "You have my word, Head Magistrate. I'll go to Vilnaria and I won't return until the problem has been resolved."

The head magistrate nodded. "Then I believe we're done here. Good luck, Amelia Huld."

Ten

It was nearly noon by the time the high magistrate and other Council members left. Before leaving, Kay and I agreed to meet Duke Gladik at the inn as planned. As Leon argued with my parents over whether or not he could return with me to Vilnaria, I slipped out of the house and walked down the street toward Wolf's Den Inn.

I still didn't know what to make of Kay. I knew he was a spy, and I knew that Sadie admired him—but little else. And now he'd be accompanying me and the duke back to Eldnaire. Could I really trust him?

"Lia!" someone shouted behind me.

I turned to see Sadie barreling toward me. She stopped inches from crashing into me, bending over as she panted, out of breath. Today, she wore a scarlet brocade gown with a matching ribbon attached to her braid.

"Sadie, are you all right?" I asked.

She gave me an incredulous look. "Am *I* all right? I'm pretty sure that's the question I should be asking *you*. My mother just told me what happened. Why didn't you say anything?"

I winced. "Sadie, I can't talk right now…I'm already late for a meeting."

Sadie glared at me. "All right, let's go then. We can talk on the way." She started walking, and I followed. "You don't even know where I'm going…"

Sadie looked back over her shoulder as she walked. "Wolf's Den Inn, right?"

I blinked. "How did you—"

"You're going to meet the duke, aren't you?" Sadie slowed her pace, allowing me to catch up and walk alongside her as she continued speaking. "Yesterday evening, you mentioned that you were going to give the duke directions—which I assume meant directions to a place where he could stay. Wolf's Den is the best inn in Averndale—without being overly expensive—so it's perfect for travelers like the duke. But my real question is, what happened during the meeting?"

I stared at Sadie. "You got all of that from one vague conversation?"

"I want to hear about the meeting, Lia."

I sighed. "All right, fine… I'll tell you."

As we continued walking through my neighborhood, I filled

Sadie in on my time in Vilnaria—how I pretended to be an ambassador, met the emperor, and left for Ivanyar. Then I told her about the meeting. The high magistrate's sentence, and the opportunity I had been given to avoid it. For once, Sadie stayed silent as I spoke. I finished explaining as we neared the inn—a large building that took up an entire block of the street at the edge of my neighborhood.

I stopped walking and turned to Sadie. "So, it seems I'll be heading back to Eldnaire after all."

Sadie watched me, her lips pressed into a line. "I can't believe that you actually met the new emperor. And they really expect you to prevent a war? That's…insane."

"Insane or not, I have to do it if I want to keep my family safe." My hand reached up to grasp the necklace Kyvir had given me. "And, of course, I'm looking forward to seeing the emperor again."

Sadie eyed me. "You are?"

I opened my mouth but shut it, glancing around. Other than a couple of people milling about the front of the inn, the area was clear. I turned back and gave Sadie a small smile. "Yes…I am." I lowered my voice, stepping closer. "And about that… Do you think you could keep a secret?"

Sadie's eyes glowed with excitement. She placed one hand on my shoulder and the other over her heart. "Give me all the details—no matter how small or insignificant—and I swear I won't tell another soul."

A burst of giddy excitement bubbled from within me, and I nearly giggled as I told Sadie about my time with Emperor Kyvir.

Sadie stared at me with wide eyes, her mouth gaping as I told her my news. "You're engaged to the *emperor?*"

"Well, not yet. It's more like we're engaged to the idea of becoming engaged sometime in the future—if all goes well. The emperor's mother thinks that marriage might help relations between Vilnaria and Myarna." I smiled. "But he's truly a wonderful person, Sadie—nothing like his father was. He's kind, thoughtful, and…" I trailed off as my thoughts turned to Kyvir's appearance. Would I sound as shallow as Sadie often did if I started listing off all his attractive features?

"I can't believe what I'm hearing…" Sadie shook her head. "My best friend, Amelia Huld, is engaged to the emperor of the most powerful country on this side of the continent."

My cheeks heated up. "I just told you, it's not official yet, and I still have to fix relations between our countries."

Sadie waved my words away. "Right, of course…" She stopped, then lit up. "You'll invite me over to stay at the palace when you're empress, right?"

"Sadie!" I squawked out. I lifted my hands to my cheeks, certain that they were about to burst into flames.

Sadie placed her hands on her hips and tilted her head to the side. "What? If Vilnarian dances are just as wonderful as you and Duke Gladik claim they are, then I want to experience one for myself. And, of course, I'd want to meet your husband," she grinned.

I choked on air. "We're not even engaged yet!" I hissed.

"Which I'm sure you'll remedy as soon as you return to Vilnaria."

Sadie's words brought me back to reality. I glanced up at the sun overhead. I was definitely late for the meeting at this point. "Sadie, I have to go—"

"I'll come too."

I smiled. "There's really no need...I'll just be discussing the trip with Kay and Duke Gladik."

Sadie nodded. "Exactly. And I've decided that I want to go with you." She started walking toward the inn's entrance.

I stared at the back of her red gown as she walked away from me, my words stuck in my throat. I forced my feet to move, hurrying after her.

"Sadie, wait!" I caught up to her halfway to the entrance. "Sadie, you can't come with us to Eldnaire."

Sadie glanced at me. "Why not?"

I blinked. "Well, because...because it's dangerous."

Sadie grasped the brass door handle and pulled it open, nodding for me to enter. I stepped inside the building, and the smells of fresh bread, tomato soup, and strawberries filled my nostrils. The restaurant portion of the inn was busy. Servers walked back and forth past the tables, taking and delivering orders of food.

"Miss Amelia!" I turned at the familiar voice. Duke Gladik waved at me from the far left corner of the lobby, near the staircase that led to the guest and meeting rooms. Kay stood next to him.

"*Benjamin?*"

I jumped at Sadie's voice in my ear. "Oh, right, I forgot to tell you, but Kay is actually—"

Before I could finish speaking, Sadie was halfway across the lobby. I groaned and followed behind.

Kay's eyes widened, and he froze as Sadie approached. "Miss Dourain?"

Sadie smiled. "I told you that you can call me Sadie. How are you, Benjamin?"

Duke Gladik looked between Sadie and Kay. "Benjamin?"

"That's Kay's real name," I explained.

Sadie whipped around to look at me. "Wait, what?"

I glanced at Kay.

"Let's continue this discussion somewhere else," he said in a low voice.

The four of us sat in one of the inn's private meeting rooms around a large meeting table. I listened as Kay explained to Sadie and the duke that he went by "Kay" in Vilnaria—and noticed that he left out the fact that he was a Myarnan spy.

"I understand," the duke said. "You were also using a false name. Like Miss Amelia."

Sadie hummed. "If everyone has been using false identities, then should I come up with a different name for myself as well?"

Kay frowned, leaning forward. "Miss Dourain, surely you weren't intending to come with us? I can't imagine your parents would be thrilled by the idea of you traveling to Eldnaire."

"That's true," Sadie admitted, "but I know they would still respect my decision. Besides, my father is supposed to be traveling to Eldnaire himself later this week. He's supposed to represent Myarna in some trade talks, so if anything goes wrong, he'll be around to bail us out of trouble."

"Even so, I believe it would be wiser for you to remain here," Kay said. "There's no telling what we'll face once we arrive in Vilnaria's royal city."

Sadie narrowed her eyes. "If Amelia feels confident that she'll be safe there, I see no reason why I shouldn't."

I played around with a loose strand of hair. I didn't feel confident at all—about anything. But at least once we were in the city, we would have Kyvir's protection. "Sadie, what about the journey there? We've already been attacked once. What if we're attacked again and you get hurt?"

Kay gave a nod. "Miss Amelia is correct. Although, with or without Miss Dourain's presence, that's still an issue we need to address," he said. "If the archer who shot me and ran off into the woods has informed his employer of his group's failure, then there may be more assassins lying in wait for us."

Duke Gladik frowned. "In that case, horseback riding and camping out in the woods again would be too dangerous…"

"Why don't we hire a carriage?" Sadie asked. "That would take care of the problem. We won't have to camp out if our drivers and horses are regularly exchanged."

"It would certainly help, but it doesn't quite solve our problem," Kay said. "Even if we hire a carriage driver, there's no guarantee that we won't be attacked again—and not just by mercenaries. Carriages attract bandits, and with Leon out of the picture and my shoulder out of commission, our odds of surviving another attack are far too low for comfort, Miss Dourain."

I frowned. "You're right…it'd be a mistake to assume we're safe—" I stopped as an idea popped into my head. An awful, horrible idea, but an idea nonetheless.

"Is everything all right, Lia?" Sadie frowned.

I nodded. "I think I might have a solution to our security problem."

Kay raised an eyebrow. "You do?"

"Yes…I do." I sighed. "I'll just need some money and a bigger mouth."

Duke Gladik laughed, tilting his head to the side. "A bigger mouth?"

I grimaced. "Yeah…so I can swallow my pride."

Eleven

*M*y hand flew up to cover my nose as the pungent smell of sour beer, rotten garbage—and who knew what else— wafted up from the stone sett streets of Averndale and assaulted my senses.

I never enjoyed visiting the entertainment district, and I *never* visited after sundown—until now. Ahead of me on the street, a group of men laughed loudly as one of them gagged and emptied the contents of his stomach onto the ground.

I smothered a cry of disgust as my nose wrinkled. I took a deep breath, holding it as I quickened my pace and stepped past the men and the mess. I ignored the slither of unease that snaked down my spine and shook up my own stomach as I walked. I swallowed hard, begging my body to keep my dinner where it belonged. The last thing the ground needed was more vomit.

The sound of music drifted down the street, emerging from Caravan Tavern, a popular dining and drinking spot for travelers, merchants, other working-class individuals, and the occasional scoundrel. Leon used to frequent the place as well, even before he was old enough to hold down a drink.

As I approached the scratched-up, rickety wooden doors, they swung open, and the music within blared out into the darkened street. A disheveled man with a scruffy beard and a frumpy woman with tangled hair stumbled out the doors, arm-in-arm, as they drunkenly sang along to the folk song, *The Dragon Stole the Mountain*. I kept my hand firmly over my nose as I entered the tavern, only to be bombarded by the twangs and strains of the fiddle, tambourine, and flute. The voices of the tavern-goers swelled in song with…varying levels of skill.

I jumped to the side as a man carrying a tray of empty beer steins almost bumped into me. If Leon had been with me, he would have made a comment about me being too short to be seen.

I stepped forward and something squelched beneath my boot. I froze, eyes wide as I looked down and nearly retched. I side-stepped away from the puce-colored pile of bile and slapped both hands over my mouth and nose. The entire tavern reeked of beer, bile, and body odor, with small strains of garlic and potato soup mixed in.

I wasn't too far from the door. I could turn around right now, leave the tavern and this horrid part of Averndale, and try to think of a better option. I started to turn but stopped. *No.* If I didn't have the strength to protect my companions, I had to find someone who did—especially now that Sadie would be traveling with us. Kay, Duke Gladik, and I had tried a few more times to convince her to change her mind and stay in Averndale, but in the end, we had to admit defeat.

Secretly, I was relieved that Sadie would be joining us. Despite all that we had been through together, Duke Gladik and Kay were more like tentative allies than friends, and right now, I needed a friend. A friend that I could trust.

"'Scuse me, sweetie, comin' through!"

I lowered my hands and leaped out of the path of a woman carrying a stack of dirty plates, stepping out of the aisle and over to what seemed to be the only empty table as I surveyed the tavern. Most of the tavern guests were sitting close to the stage where the musicians and singers were performing, but some stood right in front of the stage, dancing or raising their mugs and voices toward the ceiling. I kept my mouth shut but caught myself humming along.

I sighed, forcing myself to focus. My gaze drifted around the room, but I didn't see the man I was looking for among the people singing and clapping. My gaze turned to the customers sitting at the bar, and my breath caught. On the far side of the room, at the end of the bar, a man with raven hair and a dark red cloak sat with his back toward the stage. He spoke with one of the barkeepers—a man with a scruffy gray beard, gray hair that appeared to be thinning on top, and a furious look on his face. My eyes swept the room again, but all the other cloak-wearing individuals wore black, dark blue, or pine green. The man at the bar had to be the one I was looking for.

I let out a deep breath before stepping back into the aisle, weaving around the tables, servers, tavern goers, and piles of who-knew-what on my way to the man. As I approached, I could hear the conversation between the man and the barkeep over the singing and bustle of the rest of the crowd.

"You can't do that!" the bearded man yelled.

The man in the cloak laughed. "According to the contract you signed, I can. It's not my fault that you didn't hold up your end of our deal."

The bearded man seethed, gripping the handle of an empty beer stein in his hand. "You tricked me and you have the gall to tell me *I'm* at fault?"

The man in the cloak leaned forward in his seat. "Well, who else could possibly be at fault? You're the one who came to me for help. You're the one who signed the contract, and you're the one who didn't do what you agreed to do."

The bearded man grew redder than an overripe strawberry. His jaw clenched, and his body shook.

The cloaked man leaned back in his chair. "Now, if that'll be all, how about you get me another drink? Hold the poison, please."

"I hope you hang for this," the bearded man growled. He turned on his heel and disappeared into the back room of the tavern.

The man in the cloak laughed again. I stood still. Perhaps this wasn't the man I was looking for after all? Maybe they just looked similar. Unfortunately, there was only one way to find out.

My heart beat louder than the tambourine as I walked up, silently hoping that this rude, self-satisfied rapscallion was *not* the man I needed. I cleared my throat. "Excuse me, sir. Are you—"

"Sir? I don't think anyone's ever called me *that* before," the raven-haired man interrupted as he turned to face me. "But to answer your question, no, I'm not looking for companionship tonight—as much as I appreciate the offer," he smirked.

My mouth dropped open and my eyes widened. "What—I—no! That's not at all what I was going to ask you! I'm not that sort of woman!"

The man laughed. "My apologies then, fair lady. What can I do for you?"

I cleared my throat. "You wouldn't happen to be...are you Ivan Lidare?"

He raised an eyebrow. "That depends. Am I in trouble?"

I grimaced, tempted to use some of the vilest curses I had heard on my way to the tavern. Of course this snake-tongued scoundrel was my brother's instructor. I should have known. "No, you're not in trouble. But I am. And...I need your help."

Ivan laughed and shook his head. "I know I probably have a stellar reputation as a mercenary, but I have to admit, I'm surprised. There are at least thirty other mercenaries in town—ten of which are in this tavern right now. So why come to me?"

I took a deep breath, lifting my chin and drowning my doubts. "Because my brother has always spoken highly of you."

Ivan frowned. "Your brother?"

I nodded. "My name is Amelia Huld, and I—"

"Oh, you must be Leon's little sister. Now I'm *very* surprised," Ivan said, grinning. "The way he spoke about you made it seem as if you'd rather die than have anything to do with a mercenary."

I winced, glancing down at the tavern's hardwood floor. "To be perfectly honest, that's true. But this is important." As I spoke, the bearded barkeeper from before stalked over and slammed a beer stein down on the bar. The brown, foul-smelling liquid sloshed and spilled over the side of the stein, making a ring around the bottom of the mug. Ivan swung one leg over the other, ignoring the barkeep as he stormed off. "Oh? Do tell. Leon didn't get himself into more trouble, did he?"

My hands trembled, so I clasped them together. "He…almost died."

The smile vanished from Ivan's face. "Ah. I'm sorry to hear that. How is he now?"

"The doctor said he'll make a full recovery, but it was close. If the sword had cut deeper, he probably would have lost too much blood before we got him to the physician."

Ivan's gaze snapped to the stein. He grabbed the beer mug and took a few swigs before placing it down. "So," he turned back to look at me, "what exactly do you want me to do? Find out who did this to him? I already have a list of possible—"

"I already know who did this to him," I said, swallowing some of the anger that threatened to spew from my mouth. "What I need is protection."

He blinked. "What, you think they'll be after you next?"

"No, it's—" I stopped. Leon may have trusted Ivan, but that didn't mean that he was trustworthy or that he should know more than was necessary. "I'm on my way to Vilnaria with a group," I said. "There's someone there who will help us stop the attempted murderers, but we need to make sure that we get there safely."

Ivan groaned, slapping his palm to his forehead. "Seriously? You just want an escort?" He jabbed his thumb at his chest. "What do I look like, a novice? I'm far more suited to gathering intelligence and sneaking into places I really shouldn't be. Clashing swords with bandits or marauders is a *gross* waste of my talent."

I stared at the dark-haired man, caught between irritation and amusement. "You sound exactly like my brother…"

Ivan flashed a smile. "Well, I did teach him everything he knows." He placed a hand on his chin and hummed as he looked at me.

I stiffened under his gaze but resisted the urge to step back.

Ivan clicked his tongue and shook his head. "Okay, fine," he sighed. "You've convinced me. I'll do it."

I breathed out, closing my eyes. "Thank you…"

"Yeah, yeah. Now for the most important part. How much is in the pouch you're wearing around your neck? Because I can already tell that for escorting a group to Vilnaria, it's not nearly enough."

My eyes widened as my hand flew to my chest, where the pouch lay beneath my blouse. "How did you notice—never mind." I grabbed the pouch, slipping it out of my blouse and over my head before offering the coin purse to Ivan. "This is all that I have right now, but I promise you'll be fully compensated once we reach Vilnaria."

Ivan glanced from me, to the coin pouch, and back again. "I think I'd be more offended if I weren't aware that you've never hired a mercenary before, but you should know that only beginner mercenaries accept down payments on jobs. Seasoned mercenaries like myself always expect to be fully compensated *before* doing the job."

I frowned. "I know, but I—"

"However," Ivan interrupted, holding up a finger, "this case is a little different. Some *degenerates* decided to mess with one of my students—" he narrowed his eyes, slamming his fist on the bar counter "—and I don't appreciate that. So if I need to take on some degrading escort job and accept a down payment to make those sons of—" he cleared his throat, eyeing me. "To make them pay, I will."

Listening to Ivan, I understood my brother more than ever before. It was disturbing how much Leon had learned from this man. Leon had gone to Ivan to learn swordsmanship but had left with Ivan's entire personality.

"Well then…thank you. For your generosity."

Ivan nodded as he took the pouch from me. "Of course. I'm more than happy to help out Leon's little sister."

Behind us, some of the tavern guests broke out into a fit of raucous laughter. I glanced over at the heavily intoxicated group as my stomach turned from the sour-smelling air. I gagged and turned back to Ivan. "I…have to go," I said. "Meet us at Wolf's Den Inn at first light."

He scowled. "Can we make that second light? Or third?"

I glared at Ivan. "Please just be there."

He sighed. "Fine, fine…I'll see you there."

I nodded, turning to go.

"Oh, and Amelia?"

I turned back around. Ivan grinned at me, lifting the money pouch up. "I look forward to doing business with you."

The next day the carriage driver helped us load our belongings into the storage compartment of the coach. My mind drifted to Leon and my mother and father. After leaving the entertainment district the night before, I had gone back to the house to grab a couple of things for the trip and say goodbye. Father and Mother had both cautioned me to stay safe, and lectured me to avoid getting into any more trouble. But compared to when we had first arrived home with Leon injured, or when I was arrested and waiting to be sentenced, they acted far more like their usual calm and warm selves.

When I entered Leon's room to say goodbye, he instructed me to look in the back of his wardrobe, saying that he had a gift for me. I did as he asked and found a slim, lightweight, sheathed sword.

"I figured you might want to have this," he had said, "just in case."

Three days before, I would have refused to even hold a sword, but now, I accepted it gratefully. Leon had nearly died because I didn't know how to defend myself, and that would never happen again if I could help it.

Amelia Huld, the timid, quiet librarian, had died the day she and her brother left for Vilnaria, leaving a stranger in her place.

As we finished stowing our bags in the carriage, Sadie glanced around. "So, where exactly is the answer to the security problem that you talked about?"

I opened my mouth, but before I could respond, someone else beat me to it.

"You called?"

I turned. Ivan Lidare stood with a smirk on his ruddy face. He wore a sword on both hips. Three daggers were strapped to his chest, another was strapped to his lower thigh, and the hilt of a sword stuck out of the black bag he wore on his back.

"That's...a lot of weapons," I said, as my eyes latched onto a couple more that I had missed the first time.

"I would have brought a few more, but they would have been such a *pain* to carry around," Ivan said, walking over.

"You hired a mercenary?"

I looked to Kay, nodding. "I tried, but I couldn't think of any better options. And since he's friends with my brother, I figured he was the safest choice."

Ivan raised his index finger. "Correction, I *trained* your brother. And since he was such a good student, I've taken on this job as a favor to him."

"What? Absolutely not!" Duke Gladik whirled around to face me. "Miss Amelia, how could you hire a common *criminal?*" He glared at Ivan. "Just the other day, we were almost murdered by mercenaries, and now you want us to put our lives in the hands of one of them?"

I frowned. "I know it's not ideal, Duke Gladik, but it is necessary—and it's just until we reach Eldnaire."

"But—"

"Now is hardly the time to get into another argument." Kay crossed his arms over his chest. "We need to leave."

"Right," I said, straightening my shoulders. "I think we're ready now."

Ivan grinned. "More than ready." The mercenary whistled as he walked toward the front of the carriage to join the driver.

The duke's nose wrinkled in disgust. He frowned, turned on his heel and stalked toward the coach. "I'll be in the carriage!" he yelled over his shoulder.

"Miss Dourain."

Sadie and I turned to look at Kay. His grim expression made my stomach flip.

"What is it Ben—Kay?" Sadie crossed her arms.

Kay sighed. "I still think that you should remain in Averndale…for your own safety."

She glared at him. "If my friend doesn't have that choice, then why should I? I'm going to Eldnaire with all of you." Sadie turned and grabbed my hand, dragging me toward the carriage. "Come on, Amelia. Let's go join the duke."

I glanced over my shoulder as Sadie and I headed for the carriage. Kay stood motionless, jaw clenched, staring at the ground. My chest tightened. Even Sadie's parents had given their consent to allow her to accompany us, so why was Kay so worried? As a spy, did he know something that the rest of us weren't aware of?

Twelve

We rode all day and through the night, only stopping when it was time to exchange horses and drivers in the towns along the way. I slept through a couple of the later exchanges, despite the carriage's hard, wooden bench, and my back and neck ached painfully once I woke up in the morning.

Once everyone was awake, we stopped at an inn for breakfast, to freshen up and to make one last exchange before we reached Vilnaria.

Back in the carriage, I looked around at the others. "As soon as we arrive at the palace we need to speak to Kyvir—even if we're told he's in a meeting," I said. "If the nobles have already learned that their assassination attempt failed, they might send more. If they do, and their attempt succeeds, then…"

Images of my family filled my mind. My mother singing as she swept the house, or humming as she re-shelved the books at the library. My father smiling, briefcase in hand as he left to tutor a student. And Leon, laughing as I struggled to reach a book on a higher shelf, or trying to convince me to leave work early and go fishing with him. If I failed, or if I abandoned my mission, they'd be harmed. I clenched my fists and let out a shaky breath. "We have to get the message to the emperor before the nobles can stop us."

Sitting next to me, Sadie's eyes widened. "You really think they'll send more assassins? Even at the palace?"

"I think they'll do whatever it takes to ensure that Vilnaria goes to war with Myarna," I said, "and right now, we're the only ones who know that Myarna was framed for the murder of the Ivanyaran ambassadors. The emperor still believes that Myarna is at fault."

Sadie frowned. "And after we tell him, then what? Don't we have to give him some sort of proof before he can do anything?"

"Acting behind the emperor's back and against his wishes is considered treason in Vilnaria," Duke Gladik said, glancing between us. "At the very least, the matter will be closely investigated, and if any evidence is found, the suspected treasonists will have to stand trial before the emperor, or the emperor's appointed judge. So Miss Amelia is right. This is a problem that only the emperor can fix."

"Perhaps," Kay hummed.

My gaze turned to Kay. He sat across from me, next to the duke, looking out of the coach's small window with his arms crossed over his chest.

"What do you mean?" I asked.

Kay glanced at me. "To be perfectly honest, Miss Amelia, I find this whole situation strange. From the very beginning, Emperor Kyvir's stance on war has made him look weak, and his lack of decisive action during the last several months has done nothing to disprove that point."

I stiffened. "Emperor Kyvir has been doing his best—I've seen it for myself. His kindness isn't weakness... The people love him."

Kay nodded. "You're correct. The people do love him. But if it weren't for the support of the people, Sir Fern, the empress dowager, and prominent nobles like Duke Gladik, I doubt the emperor would still be sitting on the throne."

As he finished speaking, the carriage ran over something and jostled us in our seats. I reached out my hand, grabbing hold of the carriage and part of the curtain covering the window in an attempt to steady myself as I frowned at Kay. "And what would you have him do? Act the part of a tyrant like his father?"

Kay shook his head. "You misunderstand me. I'm merely trying to say that this whole tragedy—the deaths of the Ivanyaran ambassadors—never would have taken place if the emperor had been more reserved about his plans for peace."

I clenched the brown fabric of my dress between my fists as my toes curled over within my boots. "Well, you can't blame him for the actions of his nobles!"

Kay straightened in his seat, crossing his muscular arms over his chest. "I'm not trying to, Miss Amelia. As I said, I'm merely criticizing how he *handled* the matter." Kay glanced out the window and then grimaced, shaking his head. "Sir Fern is a smart man. I don't understand why he didn't stop the emperor from making a fool of himself."

"I'm sure the emperor will grow into his position," Sadie shrugged. "If I've learned anything from helping my mother with our family business, it's that managing and leading people can be challenging." She sighed, slumping down in her seat. "Part of me dreads the day when I'll inherit the whole business."

Another bump rocked the coach, and the wheels clattered as the carriage slowed. I moved the curtain away from my side of the window, peeking outside. My breath caught in my throat. The city gates loomed ahead, tall and imposing. I glanced back at the others. "It looks like we've finally reached Eldnaire."

After passing through the city gates, the coachman dropped us off at the city square. The square looked just as it had when Leon and I had first visited. The marketplace lay to the right, with shops and row after row of stalls adorned with colorful awnings, and merchants calling out their wares. To the left side of the square stood an ominous stone building with a bell tower placed at the top. Eldnaire's Court of Judgment.

Two gallows stood on the ground in front of the building, but unlike the first time Leon and I saw the city square, both gallows were empty.

And straight ahead, stretching the length of the city square and beyond in all its gold and glittering glory lay Eldnaire's imperial palace.

As the five of us walked across the city square, a voice called out from our right. "Sir? Sir!"

I turned. A man jogged from the marketplace, weaving through the throngs of people crowding the square.

Duke Gladik stepped forward. "Francis? Whatever is the matter? Did something happen?"

The man stopped a few feet away, panting as he caught his breath. He was a tall man with a thin frame, short, fair hair, and freckles scattered all over his nose and cheeks. "Sir! I'm so glad you're back—you're needed at the estate right away," he gasped.

Duke Gladik's eyes flickered with an emotion I didn't recognize, and he nodded. "I see…" He turned to the rest of us, words rushing from his mouth. "I apologize for leaving you so soon—but it seems I have other matters to attend to. I'll meet all of you at the palace as soon as I am able. Farewell!" He strode off, followed by Francis in the direction of the marketplace, where they were soon swallowed up by the crowds.

A sliver of unease slid its way beneath my skin like a splinter at the duke's sudden departure. I tore my gaze away from the crowds and turned back to the others.

"And then there were four," Ivan said, smiling wide. "Now, let's get you all to the palace so I can get paid."

We walked through the throngs of people wandering about the square, approaching the gates of the palace. Six guards stood at attention at the entrance.

"Is it normal for them to have so many guards on patrol?" Ivan whispered. "What are they afraid of? That someone will go and chip off a piece of gold from the palace walls?"

"No," Kay murmured. "Something must have happened while we were gone—perhaps an assassination attempt."

My eyes widened. "What?"

Kay shook his head. "Calm down...I'm sure the emperor is fine."

I frowned but nodded, letting out a deep breath as we approached the guards at the gate. A slight breeze blew strands of my hair into my face, and I brushed them back, tucking them behind my ears. Through the iron-barred gate, I spotted the rose bushes in full bloom, their vibrant crimson petals stood out against the deep green bushes and shrubs.

The guards straightened as we reached the gate. "State your name and purpose," the guard on the right said.

I stepped forward. "My name is Velia Tynan, and I've come as an ambassador of Ivanyar to speak with Emperor Kyvir."

The guards exchanged glances, and the first guard spoke again. "Well then, Velia Tynan, you're under arrest for the murder and impersonation of the Ivanyaran ambassadors."

Thirteen

"**S**o what now?" Sadie asked.

"I...I don't know," I said, staring at the straw-covered stone floor.

The two of us were in the palace dungeons. The guards at the gate had grabbed all four of us, stripped us of our belongings and had thrown Sadie and me into a cell. I hadn't seen what happened to Kay or Ivan, but I heard Ivan cursing out the guards when they were taking our stuff. My gaze drifted around the dimly lit, dank cell. It reeked of urine and wet cement. I stood in the middle of the small, rectangular area. I hadn't moved an inch since the guards first shoved us inside and locked the door. My mind felt as though it was filled with feathers. The more I tried to clear out the feathers, the more they drifted and swirled around, blocking my thoughts. For the second time in two days, I'd been arrested—but this time, the accusations were far worse and completely false.

I frowned, blinking. "I mean, obviously something happened

while we were away—the nobles must have found out Leon, Kay, and I aren't real ambassadors—maybe the mercenaries that attacked us figured it out and told them—and they decided to use that information to frame us?" My frown deepened as I examined the three stone walls of the cell. Someone had scratched tally marks into the wall, beneath the barred window.

Seven groups of five, plus two more marks. Thirty-seven. Spending one day in this stone prison was already a nightmare. Thirty-seven days sounded like torture.

I shivered and shook my head. "But everything is going to be fine," I told Sadie. "I…I'm sure that once Kyvir finds out what happened, he and Sir Fern will find a way to fix this."

"Well, maybe…" Sadie glanced through the iron bars into the outer room.

The vertical and horizontal bars spanned from the floor to the ceiling, creating a rectangular grid pattern—big enough to reach a hand or foot through, but nothing else. The door to the cell was also barred. The outer room was nearly three times bigger than our small cell. A singular wooden door stood in the middle of the wall of the outer room, with crystal torches on both sides—whose light barely reached our cell.

"Amelia, I really hope you're right, but at this point, don't you think it's possible that the emperor simply…changed his mind?"

My shoulders jerked back. "What?"

Sadie looked at me. "I mean, what if the emperor is no longer interested in cultivating peace with the north? Maybe while you were gone, he decided it was wiser to make his nobles happy instead—"

"No!" The word shot out of my mouth like a crossbow bolt, echoing off the stone walls of the cell. I swallowed, lowering my voice. "No...this was just a mistake. I doubt the emperor even knows that I'm here yet. The nobles probably bribed the guards to arrest us secretly—" I frowned. "But...those guards were imperial guards. Kay said so himself... No one other than the emperor and his highest advisers would have the power to command them to do anything..."

I had hardly finished speaking when the outer room opened and a guard entered, carrying two plates of food.

"Excuse me, could you please inform the emperor that Amelia is here?" I asked as he set the plates on the floor and slid them under the barred door.

The guard turned, walking back toward the door. "Wait!" I called as the door slammed behind him.

"Well, at least the food looks sort of edible," Sadie said, stepping over to the plates the guard had left behind.

I followed her gaze. Two bread rolls, green mush, and something that smelled like fish had been placed on the tin plate.

I stepped back, my nose wrinkling at the odor. "You're not actually going to eat that, are you?"

Sadie shrugged, plopping to the floor as she grabbed one of the plates. "There's no sense in starving ourselves."

I grit my teeth as Sadie's words sank in. Until Kyvir set us free, there was nothing we could do. "You're right...we're stuck," I murmured. I stumbled over to Sadie, sitting down next to her on the floor. She nudged the other plate over to me. I stared at the plate, steeling my stomach before grabbing a roll. It was hard as stone.

I looked up at the outer room door. Any minute now, Kyvir could burst through that door and let us out.

The sound of metal clanging against metal woke me from my slumber. I opened my eyes only to see stone and straw. My stomach dropped as I remembered where I was—the dungeon. I sat up as footsteps grew louder. Two guards walked toward the cell. Sadie also sat up next to me, yawning as she rubbed her eyes.

The guards stopped in front of our cell, and one of them took out a ring of keys.

"Are you letting us go?" I asked as the metal scraped against the lock.

The other guard laughed as the first guard opened the door, looking at Sadie. "Get up," he said. "You're wanted for questioning."

Sadie's eyes widened. "Oh…" She looked at me.

"Just tell them the truth," I whispered. "And try to get the guards to send a message to Kyvir."

She nodded, dragging herself to her feet. As she stumbled toward the cell door, one of the guards grabbed her arm as the other shut the cell door, locking it behind him before they escorted Sadie out of the room.

The outer door shut behind them with a resounding clang that echoed through the room. A shiver snaked down my spine and I shuddered. My eyes traveled around the dark cell, only illuminated by a small barred window just below the ceiling. I pulled my knees to my chest. With Sadie gone, the cell felt bare and lifeless.

A muffled shriek rang out from behind the door of the outer room. My heart froze. *Sadie.* I shot to my feet, grasping the iron bars of my cell. Sadie screamed again, louder. My head and heart pounded, my throat dried out. "Sadie!" I yelled through the bars. Sadie continued screaming, the sound pierced my ears and stabbed my heart. "Sadie!" I screamed, tugging at the bars. The screaming stopped. "Sadie!" My voice left my mouth in a screech, and echoed back at me. I sank to my knees, covering my mouth with my hands. My whole body shook, tears poured from my eyes. The silence spoke louder than Sadie's screams.

I curled up in a ball on the floor and shut my eyes, trying not to imagine what made Sadie scream like that. Or what made her stop.

Sometime later, a skittering sound reached my ears, and I sat up. It was probably a rat.

I shuddered, hugging myself tight.

The door to the outer room opened with a creak, and I turned, hoping beyond hope to see the guards with Sadie, safe and sound. Instead, a familiar figure with red hair and a mustache entered the room.

Relief rushed through me. "Sir Fern!"

Fourteen

Sir Fern's boots and cane tapped against the damp stone floor as he approached my cell. He wore a dark violet cloak that clashed against his short, red hair and complimented his black suit and gloves. "Hello, Amelia. I hope you had a pleasant journey." His voice was as smooth and gentle as a becalmed sea.

My attempt at laughter escaped my lips, sounding more like a strangled sob. "Pleasant isn't quite the word I'd use," I said, standing. "Sir Fern...the guards took my friend away—I heard her screaming. What's going on?" I swallowed hard. "The guards... the guards accused us of killing the Ivanyaran ambassadors—but why? And...how did they manage to find out who I really am?"

Sir Fern stepped closer to the cell, rubbing the large amethyst adorning the top of his cane with his gloved thumb. His eyes gleamed despite the dim light. "Well, Amelia, they found out because I told them, of course."

I blinked. "What?"

He smiled, lifting his chin. "I would never allow a group of *despicable* Myarnan assassins to get away with sabotaging relations between Vilnaria and Ivanyar. As the emperor's most trusted adviser, I had to take action."

My chest tightened and my lungs grew heavy enough to collapse within my chest. I stumbled, grasping onto the rusty iron bars to catch myself from falling. "I don't under—you told them?"

Sir Fern rested both of his hands on his cane. His smile fell, replaced with a look of concern "Amelia, I didn't have a choice. I couldn't allow you to come back and continue to deceive the emperor and all of Vilnaria."

"What are you talking about? Why are you—"

"Your plan was simple," Sir Fern interrupted. "You and your brother were sent from Myarna to assassinate the Ivanyaran ambassadors, infiltrate the palace, and provide false information to the emperor. When the nobles started to become suspicious, you summoned another associate to put everyone's suspicions aside—and it worked. After that, you and your fellow assassins were able to leave Vilnaria along with all the goods you received from the emperor and nobles. You would have gotten away with it too, but you got greedy and came back to Vilnaria for more. Little did you know, your secret was uncovered while you were gone, and everyone was prepared for your possible return."

I stared at the red-haired man, my heart beating faster than a galloping horse. The situation couldn't be clearer. Even I could understand what Sir Fern meant. "How could you do this to us?"

Sir Fern raised his brows. "How could I do what? My job? If anyone is in the wrong here, it's you and your associates." He clicked his tongue at me. "The emperor had hoped to create and foster peace with the north, but due to the actions of you and your country, it appears that war is on the horizon."

My shoulders stiffened as I glared at him. "Where is Kyvir? I want to speak with him."

Sir Fern waved my request away. "The emperor is busy with other matters. I'm afraid he won't have time to speak with you before the execution."

I froze as horror shot through me. "Execution?"

Sir Fern laughed. "You didn't think that you'd be able to keep your life after ending the lives of so many others, did you?" His eyes glinted as he looked at me. "No, you and your associates will be executed first thing tomorrow morning."

My hand flew to my chest, grasping at the air where my necklace had hung. "You can't...you can't do that."

"I assure you, I *can*," Sir Fern chuckled. "And no, unfortunately for you, the emperor will not interfere."

Panic surged through my veins. I grabbed the iron bars, squeezing them as if I could break them. "What did you do to him? What did you do to the emperor?"

Sir Fern raised an eyebrow. "Do to him? Absolutely nothing." He placed his hand over his heart. "I serve the emperor of Vilnaria wholeheartedly. I would *never* presume to betray him. I will continue to carry out his commands until the day I die."

Sir Fern seemed to be hinting at something, but if he was trying to tell me that Kyvir approved of my execution, then I refused to believe it. Kyvir would have to come down and say it to my face.

"Sadie is completely innocent in all this," I said. "You...you can't hurt her."

Sir Fern shook his head. "War is messy, Miss Amelia. Plenty of innocent people get caught in the fire. That's just the way the world works." He smiled. "You should know that better than anyone else. It was thanks to your brother that you're in this situation to begin with. So I must say that I find it quite ironic that it'll be your neck in the noose tomorrow—not his."

I was going to be sick from the rage swirling around in my stomach. "How could you do this?"

Sir Fern sighed. "As much as I'd love to sit you down over tea and explain just how helpful your death will be to Vilnaria, I have many things to do, Miss Amelia, and no time to speak with a dead woman."

"Don't I get a trial?"

He laughed. "Foreign assassins don't get trials, Miss Amelia."

My hands dropped from the iron bars, clenching into fists. I had never wished harm on anyone in my entire life—up until now. In this moment, I wanted to punch the smug, self-satisfied sneer off Sir Fern's face.

He turned and I watched as he walked toward the exit.

"You don't feel any guilt?" I asked.

He stopped, looking over his shoulder with a gaze colder than ice. "No, Miss Amelia. I see no point in guilt. Many others have done far worse than I have to keep their empires from falling. My morality is a sacrifice that I'm more than willing to pay for the sake of my country." With that, he closed the door behind him.

My hands shook. Not just my hands, but my entire body

trembled with rage. Sir Fern knew Leon and I weren't the real ambassadors, and he knew it because he was the one who had them
murdered to begin with. He had to be the one who hired the mercenaries that attacked us on our way to Ivanyar—the reason my
brother had almost died. From the very start, he had been manip-
ulating our actions. The nobles wanted war. Tucked away in their
quiet meeting rooms and dark corners, they plotted the destruction
of the north, but our real enemy had hidden in plain sight behind
kind eyes and a red mustache.

Acknowledgments

One of the things I learned back when I published my first book, *The Librarian's Ruse*, is that writing isn't a one-person occupation.

Just like it takes a village to raise a child, it takes a community to publish a book. And if you're reading this right now, you are a part of that community, so I'd like to thank you!

Whether we're friends, family, acquaintances, or we've never even met before, you've made a difference in my life just by making it this far into my book.

But there are a few people that I'd especially like to thank, because without you, this book would not exist.

First, I'd like to thank Brad Pauquette. Not only were you the one who convinced me that *The Librarian's Ruse* needed a sequel in the first place, but you worked with me throughout every step of the writing/editing process.

Second, I'd like to thank Alli Prince. You've done so much to help get this book ready for publication, and I really appreciate you!

Next, I'd like to thank my launch team. I'm overwhelmed by the amount of support and enthusiasm I received from the moment I announced the release of *A Traitor's Vow*. All of you went above and beyond with your support, and I can't thank you enough!

I also want to say a special thank you to my family—especially my mom, dad, and my aunts. You've all been such an inspiration to me, and I wouldn't be here today if it weren't for all of you.

And most importantly, I want to thank God. The one who made me and gave me such an amazing community of friends and family. The one who's always gotten me through the hardest times of my life, and the one who instilled such a deep passion for storytelling in my heart.

Thank you so much.

Thirzah

Thirzah was born in the Netherlands, but grew up in Southern Maryland. She published her first book, *The Librarian's Ruse*, in the summer of 2023.

When she's not reading or writing books, you'll find her sipping mint tea or traveling across the country. As the former managing editor of *The Pearl*, Thirzah has worked with many writers to help them improve their work. Learn more about Thirzah and her books on her website, ThirzahWrites.com.

Ready for the exciting conclusion?

The final book releases winter 2025!

An Ambassador's Ploy

Join Thirzah's free email newsletter for an alert
when it's available!

ThirzahWrites.com/AnAmbassadorsPloy
Or scan this QR code

Did you read the first book?

Don't miss the beginning of Amelia's exciting adventures
The Librarian's Ruse
Available from all major retailers

www.ingramcontent.com/pod-product-compliance
Lightning Source LLC
Chambersburg PA
CBHW020655180626
46816CB00003B/1294